Fiction International 53
Algorithm

D1379153

Fiction International is a journal of arts and culture published at San Diego State University. *Fiction International* was founded, published, and edited by Joe David Bellamy at St. Lawrence University from 1973 to 1982.

Business correspondence, including that related to subscriptions and advertising, should be directed to:

Harold Jaffe
Editor, *Fiction International*
Department of English
San Diego State University
5500 Campanile Drive
San Diego, CA 92182–6020

E-mail: fictioninternational@gmail.com

Cover image "Void" by Sophie Calhoun
Cover design by Thomas Gresham & Kurt Kroeber
Back cover image by Kenneth Calhoun

Journal typeset by Norman Conquest Design Lab (Redding, CA)

ISSN 0092-1912
ISBN 978-0-931362-18-7

Call for Submissions: Compassion

Fiction International is accepting submissions for issue theme: Compassion. Submissions will be accepted online or through mail from October 1, 2020 to February 15, 2021. We consider submissions of fiction, non-fiction, visuals, and indeterminate texts reflecting the theme. Online submissions must be submitted through Submittable at **fictioninternational.submittable.com/submit**. Hard copy submissions must be printed out, accompanied by an SASE, and mailed to:

Harold Jaffe
Editor, *Fiction International*
Department of English
San Diego State University
5500 Campanile Drive
San Diego, CA 92182–6020

We exercise all due care in handling manuscripts, but we cannot be responsible for loss. Please allow one to three months for reply. If submitting through Submittable or mail isn't possible, we may accept emailed submissions **providing you receive approval in advance**. Should you have any questions, please email the editor at: **hjaffe@mail.sdsu.edu**.

Subscriptions

Fiction International is published once yearly. Annual subscriptions – Individuals: $16 plus $2 postage for U.S. / $16 plus $4 postage for international addresses. Institutions: If subscription is issued through a subscription service, their terms and rates apply. Otherwise, the rates are: $35 plus $2 postage for U.S. / $35 plus $4 postage for international addresses. Some past issues are also for sale. Please see our website (**fictioninternational.sdsu.edu**) for a complete list of available past issues and prices. Remember to add applicable postage when ordering.

Use of FI in the Classroom

Please consider assigning this issue (or one of the past issues) as part of your reading list. Ask your bookseller to contact Harold Jaffe (hjaffe@mail.sdsu.edu) for information on availability of multiple copies.

Donating to FI

Although we maintain an office at San Diego State University, *Fiction International* is 100% independent of financial aid from the university. Outside of sales and subscriptions, our continued existence relies on supporters who make cash donations. That is why we are asking people who support the artistic merit of the journal and the progressive political thinking it advances to support Fiction International by making a tax-deductible donation. If you would like to donate to Fiction International using a credit card, please visit our website (fictioninternational.sdsu.edu) and use the "Donate" button to link to our PayPal account. You may also mail a check to: *Fiction International,* Department of English, San Diego State University, 5500 Campanile Drive, San Diego, CA 92182-6020

Support FI Online

Fiction International maintains an active online presence through its website, Twitter, and Facebook. Please support us by visiting the following addresses and by recommending us to family and friends.

fictioninternational.sdsu.edu
twitter.com/FictIntl
facebook.com/FictIntl

Contents

7	**em fowler** Special Delivery
8	**Jaiden Dokken** Compliancy
11	**Brett Stout** Sometimes a Lunatic, Mostly a Heretic
12	**S. Bennett** Endos Fifty
16	**Carrie Seidler** An Invocation of Glory
21	**Ron Burch** The Name of the Dog is Death
22	**Rosalind Goldsmith** What Is -?
37	**Robert J. Cross** Datagrid
40	**Eric Blix** Heterogeneous Nothing
55	**Charles Joseph Albert** The Copy
58	**Kon Markogiannis** Grafik 15
59	**Toby Olson** Nora's Research Club
65	**Kathleen Heil** If Lost, Please Call
67	**Marilyn Stablein** Sequence
68	**Barbara Lock** The Toxicant
75	**Text Greshan** Nikki
81	**D. Harlan Wilson** Velvet Sunshine
90	**Alex Checkovich** '71's
96	**Ngozi Oparah** Swallow
110	**Fabio Tasso** Reproduction
111	**KKUURRTT** Advanced Praise
112	**Kenneth Calhoun** The White Woman
118	**Ben Miller** it all melts down to this: a novel in timelines (chapter 17)
119	**Stephen-Paul Martin** The Phantom Zone
138	**Robert Boucheron** The Streckfuss-Hamadi Algorithm
143	**Cassandra Passarelli** Fifty-One Rolls
151	**Dan Moreau** Find X
152	**Matthew James Babcock** Forms I & II
160	**Kevin Cocozello** Why I Write 1.0
161	**Hannah Kauders** A Pragmatic Analysis of the Subjunctive Mood in a Breakup Letter
166	**Harold Jaffe** Dada

Jaiden Dokken

Compliancy

No lusting, thrusting, no hot breathed gasps or fingers curled in my hair, just a youngish white presumably CIS straight man telling me he's been slingin' IUDs all day everyday since Trump was elected, like this is something funny, like not wanting to be pregnant is an impulsive reaction to a political climate. Which it is and it isn't, but I've been trying my best to trick this sweet body of mine since I was 15 years old, letting fake hormones lie and pretend pregnancy, which is very clever medicine. 15 is young though, so is 16 17 18 so is 23 and I'm just over here with my head on some crinkly fucking paper pulled taut, feet in those goddamn stirrups, this dude staring right into me telling me it probably won't hurt that much while his penis lays safe and limp between his legs not lit up under these fluorescent lights. And of course it hurts. No pain medications, freezing cold room, an apathy saved especially for womxn. I tell him it hurts and he tells me to relax and I think I might vomit and my vision starts to blur and I hope to pass the fuck out but of course I don't, not yet, not until it hurts so bad that I'm crying and finally when he says all done he pulls his gloves off finger by finger snap snap snap and walks out of the room and everything goes dark. I wake up to a round kind-faced womxn standing by my shoulder holding a cold washcloth to my forehead asking if I'm okay, if I know where I am, and I can't talk for some reason but she knows this and touches me lightly and even in this stupor I'm certain the youngish white presumably CIS straight man is in the next room doing this to another womxn, prowling from room to room leaving sad clammy patients in his wake, ushering in mother-like womxn to clean up his desperate little messes, coax us into leaving, freeing up that chair so he can keep on slingin'. So I play my part, stumble off that crinkly paper, and surrogate-mom steadies me when I see stars. She leaves the room while I get dressed which feels absurd considering they just inserted a piece of plastic farther into my body than anything else has ever gone but I suppose there isn't anything intimate about what we did, just a necessary invasion, but while I stumble trying to shove my leg through the tube of these pants I feel something hot and needy drip onto my hand and I realize I'm crying again. I'm terrified to bend too much because everything hurts and getting dressed takes a while. I leave the room expecting round kind-faced womxn to be waiting outside but she's not so I wander to the check-out desk and the person tells me I can leave so I do and when I step outside there's a silver subaru waiting for me and I carefully fold myself into it. Earlier this person I love told me he'd pick me up and I said no I'll walk because I'm a #coolgirl and also things are strained between us but when I walk out and see him I'm grateful for his solid warmth, steady gaze, the way he always smells like tea tree toothpicks. He pulls out chocolate peanut butter gelato, red wine, and a bottle of ibuprofen and I still feel like crying so I mutter a quiet thank you and try not to move my body, think about my body, feel my body. Later I'm in the bathroom scared to pee or shit because I'm almost certain I'll eject this IUD right into the toilet, ripping my insides the whole way out like a bloody streamer and all this trauma will be for nothing. In these minutes of mustering my bravery I consider the pain I'll endure to not get pregnant, to not create a perfect distillation of love and life, to not have to look into my child's eyes while the world burns around them, to not have to answer them when they ask me why the fuck I chose to birth a human when their survival is impossible. I sit on that toilet mourning the babies I'll never carry, the trimesters I'll never spend staring at my full belly, a lover's hand cupping it with smiling lips pressed to my neck, mourning the moments wasted daydreaming my perfect family: sleepy morning cuddles tiny giggles and heads that smell sweet, hopeful voices that call me momma. Mourning that this isn't a choice, that I have no option but to be a womxn that doesn't want to birth children, mourning that previous mothers and fathers took this option from me and at age 23 I'm just trying to figure my life out, and I don't want to be pregnant I just want to have sex and so I have to go through all this bullshit and now here I am cowering in my filthy bathroom afraid to take a piss, but finally I do and when I wash my hands I don't look in the mirror. I just walk out and slink into my spot on the couch, bottle of red wine half empty on the floor, surrounded by men that I love but feeling far away, feeling alone and angry and sad and wondering why no one told me it would be this bad, wondering why I feel violated when I literally asked for this, why I feel broken when everyone else seems to feel empowered by this, why it makes me depressed that my poor body thinks it's holding a special little someone when it's actually just a T-shaped piece of plastic, like watching a crow carry a piece of shiny trash around thinking it's valuable, gently tucking it into its nest.

Lud·dite *n*

1 Somebody who opposes technological and industrial innovation

Endos Fifty

On top of the cat's head, the fur and skull was gone—dermostroben—exposing mounds of pinkish crenelated tissue, the animal's brain. Protruding from its ears like glistening antennae were sensors, long probes from which dangled 300-ohm lead wires wound together in an electronic nest.

Ord sent a holographic image, luminous and pulsing, to the Creon Five sector, but first he suppressed its audio. He squelched spectrums 6 through 16 to eliminate the horrid miaul and hissing of the creature and reduce the sputter of its throat saliva which caused static in the sensor tract.

Ord telemined through the outer tunnel and atmosphere corridor, pausing briefly at Creon Four to straighten the gold tube-fusion band around the circumference of his spherical body. He pushed it over his eyes, white with gray irises, typical of his kind who had also been exposed to the fluorine and radiation of THE CLOSENING, when the third sun burst. He liked the tube-fusion just above his retractile lids, so that when it glowed, the yellow light reflected off his beak and glinted, as in the ancient portrait of Warrior 7-Kryak.

Finally, Ord was ready.

In Creon Five, as usual, Artcephalus bobbed in the enzymatic solution chamber—a shimmering pyramid 75% full of liquid—continually bathing his jowl gills which had become hard and mucous-encrusted with age. Artcephalus was 412 years old, or even older in years of the first sun.

The cat hologram had reached him intact. It hovered below his basin, throbbing and twitching.

"Ord-mato," Artcephalus telepathed, using the suffix "mato" reserved for formal occasions and discussions of fate. "From which planetoid did the feline sample arrive?"

Ord felt a tingle at the top of his sphere, where many thousands of years ago his ancestors had scards, blankets of tiny waving tentacles which now existed only in the mutant intrabirths. All scard sensation was supposed to have been extinguished after the sixth generation—and Ord had never revealed that his endos tingled… "Specimen is from EARTH, sub-capture of biped hirsute bellicose humanoid Z-type, gender independent. It is one of their experimentations."

A stream of excretory bubbles passed through the enzymatic solution while Artcephalus pondered.

Ord could feel his tube-fusion had slipped down over his scalp, but he didn't telekine it back into position—and of course he wouldn't wattle it back. In the year Minus 211, Artcephalus had terminated, by asphyxiation, six elders for vainglory.

"We shall follow *The Determiner*," declared Artcephalus.

Ord blinked a formal affirmation. The Determiner specified that alien life forms could be utilized for experimentation, even in the most expansive and dire manner, if to do so was exemplified by the alien planet's own belief system or practices.

"Precisely what are Earth's regulations on animal experimentation?" Artcephalus inquired.

"Officially, in statutes, Earth rulers specify testing on animals only when necessary, with requisite pain minimization protocol during research." Ord felt the doubt and annoyance from Artcephalus and saw the clouded enzymatic solution near his pole endos—so Ord kept relaying, in a rapid stream, "But these felines evidence the contrary, and evince trumpost. Their skull separations are part of an IRB/FDA-approved, pharmacologically-funded experiment to study the effects of aerosol paint fumes on graffiti criminals in ghetto areas of the Earth-bord."

Artcephalus' eyes lightened and became almost clear. He was happy. "Yes… Even though Earth regulation forbids it, in practice animal life forms have been used for unnecessary, painful experiments. And the administration has lied about it… Thus we may experiment on Earth life forms without violating The Determiner..."

Ord blinked again, a slow watery slide of his lids to show total concurrence.

Artcephalus' fusion tube glowed; he was calculating. "From a warm climate, but light-skinned. Pink living tissue—remove all body hair by villosear, pubic regions by hirsear, and lubricate. Place all humanoid subjects in the Outer Zone to observe their dermablistering, aura-prote decimation rates, and life-decay matrices. Thus we shall calculate the deterioration of our atmosphere and its radio-flourine levels. Fifty thousand humanoid biped samples shall be necessary, for exactitude. When can they be obtained?"

"In sixteen hexos," Ord telepathed. He stared for a moment at the cat hologram which had stopped pulsing and writhing. The cat lay on its side, legs splayed, tongue dangling, eyes closed.

Galaxies away, the animal had expired.

Carrie Seidler

An Invocation of Glory

It Is

Drywall, wood panel frontage, foam fill, Naugahyde, gold-plated upholstery nails.

Drywall is primarily composed of Gypsum, which grows like transparent grass in ancient lake beds. The water molecules in gypsum are crystallized; when heated, they vaporize and cool the wall board, thus making it fire-resistant. Gypsum itself is a mature alignment of bassanite crystals which seek one another out, lining up like a pearl necklace to form crystals; an occurrence observed by Professor Liane G. Benning from the University of Leeds, who described it as being "caught in the act of assembly."

The Gypsum is then mixed with pulped oak from the Moravsky Krumlov forest. Birthed via acorns. At the time of harvesting, the wood had been pocked by an eclipse of ravenous gypsy and nun moths.

The business-facing wood panels are spruce, 60 years old, felled in the Bohemian forest, but milled in Moravskoslezský, over 500 kilometers away. This inefficient system was created by an agreement between the Bohemian-Moravian Confederation of Trade Unions and the Czech Republic National Forestry Commission.

The panels have been Resin coated and cleaned with lemon scented Mop All, (from Hranipex!).

The Naugahyde is imported from Connecticut. It is a composite of knit fabric backing, aka rayon, which is made of cellulose, sourced from upland cotton fields in Lubbock, Texas, which is then coated with expanded polyvinyl chloride (PVC) plastic manufactured in Houston. The coating is burgundy, of the same variety favored for upholstering dive bar stools in the Rust Belt in the late 1960s.

The foam fill was drawn out of the back of an old floral-print couch in the manager's office. It was bought at an estate sale in Hřebeč along with two brass lamps and a mountain dulcimer.

The leg shackles are a composite of seat belts from a 1998 Škoda Octavia, and leather restraints, stolen from the Ploskov Farmyard in Lány.

The upholstery tacks are steel, imported from Thailand.

The tacks have been actively assembled in an arc across the top of the hole, resembling a chart of moon phases.

The feel is cold, smooth, occasionally sticky, crinkled at the corners, uneven grooves like a finger bent to beckon.

It smells of ammonia, lube, whispers, latex, sweat, a hint of blood, semen, vanilla, rubbing alcohol, beer, vodka, caramel coloring, grunts, baby wipes, plastic.

It radiates with traces of plutonium from the plants in Dukovany and Temlin, brought in like sand in the cuffs of engineers.

You Are

Active crystals. Lobbing rainbows. Assembling.

You are a purveyor of pleasure, a source of income, an absence, a presence, a moment, a series of pumps, a conveyance, a looking glass, a spy glass, a doorway, a connection defined by lack thereof; a rush, a worry of germs, bacteria, disease, a risk, a lowered voice, a group of chortles, a clink of glasses, a shake of heads, a dismissal.

You are probably into it, probably numb, probably huffing glue right at this moment. I bet you like it more than cleaning toilets, I bet you have no education, I bet it's fine. Everything is fine.

Thou Art

The Spirit of energy, of consciousness, collecting here, in this vacuum, in this absence.

Thou art hallowed hollowed howled. Sepulcher of carnal desire.

Thou art the god of cognitive dissonance. Well, it's not real leather, well she maybe likes it, well she maybe doesn't care, well she's probably a drug addict, she's probably high, I wish I could use *two* condoms, heck of a deal, boy oh boy, heck of a deal.

Thou art Captain of Industry, pistons, 'private part deco.' Thou art ancient, lacustrine, nymph; dryad, lubed, like piston, like engine. Thou art the useful dairy cow with metal suckers on teets, pain and milk and blood and pus. Thou art the failure of communism. Thou art the Velvet Revolution condensed and served warm like canned milk.

Thou art the goddess of acquiescence. Thou art dark matter. Thou art particle of God.

Thou art the veil of collective consciousness, ruched at a crossroads. Thou art the devil's fiddle. Thou art all of humanity coalescing in one absence.

Thou art humanity expressed by wiping itself clear.

Thou art a mirror by way of denial of mirrors.

Thou art the blessed mother and shame-ed whore.

Thou art every woman I never got to fuck.

Thou art memory.

Thou art artifice.

I Am
The spirit of crystals, the dynamism of molecules aligned. I am the wisdom of ancient lakes, now dried. I am the possibility of an acorn. I am the strength of steel forged in a looming factory, I am gold paint dipping.

I inhabit absence. I am multitudes. Trickster, prankster gods and goddesses woven like rayon threads, held in place by gold flashes of memory, filling vessels like the Tao, and the Lube.

I am energized by traces of plutonium. I am conscious by collection, I observe you. You are Schrödinger's cum. I am the kaleidoscope of deities twirling around cocks. I am the physics of thrust.

I am the head of a pin on which throbs the membrane of difference between organic and inorganic. Naugahyde and leather. I osmose through the consciousness of darkness, dredged from the earth, black juice of dinosaur bones, crystals ground to powder and slapped between sheaths of dead oak flesh to create barriers that I alone traverse. I am the parabola of space-time fabric. I am the reason no two objects can ever truly touch. I am Higgs. I am Boson.

I am barbs in your hood like South African rape condoms. I cannot be washed off. I am memory. I am unerasable. When you lie dying of prostate cancer, and flick your carousel of memory slides, you will see summer lawns, and your smiling children, and your vomiting children, and lemonade, and wedding cake. You will see the trout you caught in Lake Michigan. You tried to filet it to impress your cousins and found it was full of tiny bones; but you sat there patiently, delicately, eating around them because you were so damned proud.

Then you see yourself, crotch to wall, holding _____'s leg with one hand, vodka/
Coke in the other. You smell the pine resin and chemical approximation of lemon.
You think of your last girlfriend, then the one who put a finger up your ass to help
speed things along. You wish there were a hole *behind* you for *that*. A finger sticking
out, eager, trustworthy, no hangnails. Perfection.

I am the absence into which you thrust.

I am Glory Hole.

Ron Burch

The Name of the Dog is Death

That's the only name it responds to, said the Tech. The man was surprised but accepted the dog. He knew that the name might be a problem, so he immediately gave it a new name. The dog didn't respond to it. Mark. Hey, Mark, he said to the dog. The dog still ignored him. The man said Mark twenty-five more times, counting in his head. The dog ignored him. When the man arrived home, he told his two children, a boy and a girl, that the dog's name was Mark, but the dog wandered off to sniff the yard and refused to come into the house. The man confided to his wife that the dog's real name was Death. Good god, that's horrible, she said. The man nodded. We could never call him that in front of the kids. The man agreed and said he and the kids would make up a new name. That night they produced a list of new names for the dog. Mel didn't work. Neither did Seymour. Rags was out. The dog cocked its head at Moppet but ignored it thereafter. Sam, Sally, and Sister were all flat. After an hour, the kids grew bored and ran to their games to kill things. The man was determined to give the dog a new name. Your name is Mark, he commanded. The dog ran outside, hard to see in the failing light. Oh for god's sake, the man said. It was getting worse with the dog becoming more disobedient. The man was afraid that if he couldn't give the dog a name, it might turn to trouble. He couldn't give up the dog. It was theirs. Outside, the dog was moving into the dark of the sky, and the man whispered to it, knowing he shouldn't, "Death." He couldn't see the dog, it had grown so dark, but he heard noises in the brush and found that dog again at his side. Why can't you answer to Mark? the man asked. After that, the man may have been cruel to the dog. He became obsessed with the notion of giving it the name. But it became a misery around the house and the man grew to understand that there are some names you may never change no matter how much you love them.

Rosalind Goldsmith

What Is –?

What could evolve from this moment? This, and only this moment? Spiritually, I mean.

You don't know until you try. Think about it. Try.

Nothing endures.   There is only this moment. This.

A shooting in L.A. Twenty-four people.

Emoluments violation. This is corruption, isn't it? It might be, it might not.

Heat dome. Forty-four degrees outside, fifty-six on the bus. Choking.

Iceberg cracking, calving off.

Dead body, face slashed down one side.

Electric scooter. Flying motorcycle. Hoverboard.

This is: 1968, Detroit. Riots in the streets.

This is: kitten patting nose of Golden Retriever. Cute. Awwww.

He said: broken neck – cut down to earth.

Trees shade a fountain in the square. Mist rising. People as shade as shadows dance in the mist.

Forty-eight degrees in the shade. Fifty-six on the bus.

In-depth analysis: that statement is, seems to be. A lie? An out and out lie? Can't anyone see this? It appears to be. But.

Pet piglet running through the hedge. Snouty nose. Snuffle snuffle.

Cat playing with – an owl? Oh no. Haha. Cute. Awwwwww.

This is: corpse face down on the street. Fighting-mad crowd. Black masks. Mists of gas, some kind of gas. People running in drifting mists of tear gas.

The past: does not exist. There is only: this moment. This moment only.   This.

Try it. It is a spiritual journey. You will see.

Teen bot explains: acne diagram of how. How acne happens.

Teen bot loves: new shampoo. You will too.

Teen bot winks. Lighty eyes blinking. Likes: 2,003. Subscriptions: 847. For you.

Please. What is –?

Flying motorcycle hoverboard bird

What kind of bird? Bird screams. Eats a peanut. Hahaha. Cute.

Howls of hatred. Screaming back and forth. People dressed in black. Carrying signs. An army between two crowds. Riot shields. Seems to be: police or soldiers? No difference. None. No difference.

This is: Miami. Flooded.

This is: Marshall Islands. Flooded.

This is: Venice. Flooded.

Cockatoo swearing, seems to be English. Sounds like: Fuck this! Fuck it! Fuck you! I can't do it! Fuck! Toyota Corfu!   Wings flapping

Freak storm cell in Pittsburgh. Downed trees. House collapsed.

Weeping neighbour: "I never saw her after that."

Wings flapping.

Eighteen people in a small town in Pennsylvania. Mass shooting of – by?

What is: Incel?

What is: 8chan?

Old footage. Of: A wall. Of: A train.

Of: this moment. Nothing but this moment. This.

What could become of us if there is no past? Think about it. Try it. It is a spiritual journey.

White cockatoo flies across room, picks up red plastic bird. Walks sideways under a table. Drops plastic bird. Breaks it. Oh no!!

Movie star looks sketchy grainy. Drugged? Is was appears to be: dead?

Prisoner smiles. Says: I stabbed her in the lower back twenty-one times. I didn't feel a thing.

Blood all over the floor. Blood. The carpet stained.

He says: It was the happiest time of my life. He she walking hand in hand Chelsea Knightsbridge. Down the street round the corner.

Broken

In a house belonging to –

In a house built by –

In a house demolished by the wind, carried away by floods

In a house locked up by their father

Blood. Streaks of it. On her hand. Blood. All over. Carpet stained.

Your best face. Glowing. You *can* go out tonight! Fresh and simple to apply! See?

Like. Love. Subscribe.

What is: Evolution?

What is: Flat Earth Society?

What is: Jet stream?

Can anyone see this? It's clearly a lie. If you actually read the –

In-depth analysis.

Is was appears to be

Who can predict?

Nostradamus. Who was?

Rasputin. Entertained the ladies. Was charismatic.

What is: Charisma?

Who were: the Romanovs?

Where is: Christina Aguilera?

Cockatoo running down hallway, says in apparent English, seems to say: I can't do it. I can't do it. Runs back and forth. Screaming in apparent English: Beef the porcupine! Fuck! Good bird.

Children dancing in the light, in the rising and falling mists of water in the afternoon. As shades as shadows. Forty-eight degrees in the shade. Fifty-six on the bus. Choking.

What is: Evolution?

Who was: Nietzsche?

What is: Nihilism?

Mass of people. Mass. A single salute. Mass. The entire nation. Smashed windows. Broken glass. Smashed windows.   What is –?

Who was: Goering?

Who was: Eichmann?

Who starred in the Great Escape?

Who played Hitler in Downfall?

Planet X is heading for Earth. Uh-oh.

You can achieve spiritual evolution if you ignore the voices that tell you it's not possible. You can.

Now. Now. Now. Now. Now. You see? No past no future. Only this moment.   This.

Do you feel hatred? Do you feel self hatred? I know I do at times. And when I do, I simply take a deep breath, and – it's a spiritual journey, you see. A deep breath takes you into the present moment and holds you there. There is no past. There is no past. Only this moment. This.   What is –?

What is that?

Boy crushing skull of rabbit. Or small dog. Why does boy do this?? No: it is a cat, a raccoon, a squirrel. A living creature. Crushed.

Is was appears to be

Meaning

I shot her from two feet.

Your mother.

Yes.

Did she know?

No.

Did you say anything?

No.

Did you feel –

No.   Nothing.

It is not that difficult. Your problem is you stop half way up the mountain. Can you see that, sir?   Looks, appears to be: baffled.

You need to: Look forward. Stand straight. Take a step. Move ahead. Move up.

For God's sake.

It is not that difficult. Why can't you –?   Please?

There is no past.   There is no past.

Broken.

Cockatoo runs under table. Will not go to the vet. Oh no!! Grumbles in apparent English:

The fork is managing to be a spleen for thou. Fuck. Good bird. Good bird.

If you try this nutritional supplement once a day, your cancer will be cured in two weeks.

Like. Love. Subscribe.   Please?

Why did you kill her?

I don't know.

You don't know.

I don't know.

Broken.

Snake fish crawling up the shore on all fours. Fish – walking?

What is: Evolution?

Where is: Appalachia?

What is: Hillbilly?

Jethro swimming in the cement pond. Cows and goats in the tennis court.

Mr. Drysdale is: upset.   Miss Hathaway says: Do something.

Little boy lying face down in the sand. Arms stretched out.

This is: an angel asleep. An angel dead. An angel forsaken.

Hahahahahahahaha! Laughs in a can.

In-depth analysis. Can anyone see it? It's an absolute lie. Why can't anyone –? *See?*

What is –?

Who killed JFK? Was it the same person who killed Jeffrey Epstein?

Obviously: it was.

The people the Clintons knew. All of them dead. All involved in the

conspiracy.

If you think the earth is round you haven't looked at it lately. Just look at it. It's flat.

For God's sake. It's not that difficult. Stand up. Move forward. Use your eyes.   See.

Planet X. Uh-oh.

The cat leaps up to swat the owl. Oh no! Now the owl and the cat sit together.

So cute. Cuteness itself. Cutest baby animals. Ever. So. Cute. Awwwwwww.

This is: the body: check it: the face slashed down one side. A gash. Blood.

Is was appears to be

Broken   broken

I did it because I was depressed.

In the stream a bear wading, holding a fish.

I did it because it felt like the right thing to do.

Fish with legs crawls up the shore.

I did it because I could.

Fish evolved: into: snake fish.

This is: 1944. Train approaches. Rails lead to archway. Tall grass iron gate. People on train, getting off train. People lining up outside train.   What is –?

A man says: they did not look human they said to us: Leave. Go away. You cannot help us here. I thought they were not human. They did not look human. Not to me. An old woman was beaten on the street. To death. I saw this. It was hell. [1]

If it was not hell, what was it? Think about this. This:

Think: If it was not hell.   What was it? What was it?

SpongeBob Squarepants.

Curb Your Enthusiasm

Vicky Pollard

_____
[1] Taken from an interview in "Shoah", 1985. Claude Lanzmann

Who is: Vicky Pollard?

Who is: Matt Lucas?

Between Two Ferns.

This is: a travel opportunity. Book it. Check in. Stow your luggage
and relax. An inner journey. A spiritual awakening.

It's possible if you don't listen to the voices that tell you it's not.

Is was appears to be: Meaning

Singer falls, picks herself up, staggers – skin and bone. Looks sketchy looks drugged.

Is was appears to be: dead?

This is: 1985. Chernobyl. Game of Thrones. Nagasaki.

Britain's Got Talent.

A child singing: Nessun Dorma.

Body face down. Check it. Face slashed down one side. Blood.

Broken   broken

I did it because she was annoying me.

She was your mother.

I know that.

She's dead now.

I know that.

Do you think you had a right to kill your mother?   Meaning?

She was – I was – depressed I mean.

Cockatoo runs back and forth squawking. Refuses to go to the vet. Oh no! How will he go to

the vet?? Kitten curls up by owl. That is so cute. Ever. So. Cute. Awwwwwww.

          Slash across the face. Body face down.

Man says: I go back thirty-five years. This is what I saw. They were not human. I thought: they

could not be human. She died in the street. It was hell.[2]

If it was not hell   What was it?

What was it?   For God's sake   What was it?

Woman sits by chain link fence, weeping weeping: my child my child, mi hija – I don't know

where she is – there are people who –wings flapping flapping.   This is: What is?

     It's just not – can't anyone see? An obvious lie. Can't anyone see it?

     For God's sake. It is not that difficult. Why can't anyone *see?*   Please?

                    Broken   broken

What is – who is – how can –

          And now this: an in-depth analysis – of:

Kitten sits on a dog's head. Cute. So cute. Ever. So. Cute. Awwwwww.

[2] Taken from an interview in "Shoah", 1985. Claude Lanzmann

This is: Chicago 1968

This is: New York 2001

This is: Paris 1912

This is: New York 1929

This is: Belgium 1915

This is: Appalachia 1935

What is: catastrophic equivalence?

What is: Trench Warfare?

Where is: Verdun?

What is: the Maginot Line?

Look at that squirrel! He's eating a peanut! Cute! Awwwww.

In a house torn apart by the wind –

In a house locked up by the father

In a house seized by the bank –   Meaning   meaning

Blood. Streaks of it. On her hand. Blood. All over. Carpet stained with blood.

Is was appears to be   Please.

I can't tell you I did anything wrong. Because I didn't.   Meaning

He was – do you understand? Charismatic.   Meaning

There is no past no future. It is a spiritual evolution. Just this moment. This.   Meaning

Blood on the floor. Carpet stained.

Broken   broken

There is no past, you see. It is not that difficult, sir. Try. There is just this moment. This.

For God's sake.   Please?

We need an in-depth analysis of –

Don't you think –?

Can't you see that –?

Cockatoo flapping wings screaming and will not go to the vet. Oh no! Catch him! Oh no! the

curtains! He will tear the curtains!

What is: Scientology?

What is: Nexium?

What is nihilism?

Who was: Rasputin?

Who were: the Spice Girls?

How many people died in World War One?

Planet X. Uh oh.

Yellowstone caldera. Uh oh.

What was: World War Two?

Who starred in the Great Escape? Who?

Where is Christina Aguilera? Where?

Body face down. Check it: face slashed. Blood. Carpet stained with blood.

There is no past. It is a spiritual journey. Now. Now. Now. Now. Now.

Do you feel hatred? Do you feel self hatred? Do you feel hatred sometimes?

Take a deep breath. Breathe into the present moment.

There is only this moment.   This.   It is a spiritual journey.

Book it. Like it. Love it. Subscribe.

Think.

Try.

See.

It is not that difficult –

Think.

Think.

Think.

What is –?

What is –?   Please?

–broken?

Why can't anyone – *see*?

Who played Phoebe in Friends? Who?   For God's sake. Try.

In a house belonging to – meaning

In a house torn down by the wind – meaning

In a house locked up by their father – meaning

Broken broken broke en.

```
1 D A T A G R I D 8     T H E 8 W O R L D 8
7 4 9 8 9 4 8 4 8 2     M U S T 9 L E A R N
0 B Y 8 6 8 3 4 3 6     O M O D E R N I T Y
5 6 3 8 1 1 7 7 2 0     S L O V E 1 H A 5 0
3 R O B E R T O 5 7     B E C O M E 8 1 M A
6 2 8 6 2 1 3 5 4 4     G I N A R Y 3 D E A
8 J A M E S S 2 6 0     D 6 I N 7 T H E 6 E
4 6 2 8 1 8 9 0 2 4     Y E 5 8 0 F 9 Q U A
4 C R O S S O 7 2 0     N T U M 7 C I R C U
4 1 8 9 3 9 1 1 3 7     I T R Y 3 T H E 3 0

P P O S I T E 9 O F     N F L I C T 3 V I O
7 F A M I L I A L 2     L E N C E 4 A G A I
I S S C O L L A P S     N S T 8 T H E 4 U N
E 6 1 N 1 T H E 2 A     R E A S O N A B L E
S H E S 7 O F O T H     3 G E N I U S O I S
E 2 O L D 1 W O R L     6 E X C E S S 5 4 O
D 6 D E S T R U C T     N L Y 2 A N S A R R
I O N B E Q U A L S     A Y 2 O F B T R A U
4 P E A C E O R E A     M A S O C A N 7 R E
S O N 9 M U S T 3 1     V E A L 3 T H E 3 O
```

```
VERSIGHTSB   URTBADDICT
MAN8HAS4TO   ION8PUSHES
O4LONG3BEE   OITS6NONEN
N6BLINDEDO   TITY1INTOO
BY9THE8CHA   THEIREALIT
SM8OF1THE4   Y2OF2THE4U
SUBCONSCIO   SER2THOSEO
US2DESIRE4   WHO8SUFFER
BLEEDSOINT   4FROM2PRET
O1FUTURE3H   ENSIONITOꓵ

REVOLUTION   PAINOTHE8W
ꓹWILL4BEBL   ORLD9MUST2
EFT8CLINGI   BREAK8FREE
NG3TO1THEO   SFROM1STAG
EMBERS8OFꓹ   NATIONBORꓹ
ORDER1PARA   SUCCUMBSTO
NOIAꓹPREPA   8THEꓹHORDE
RES8ONEOFO   SGOF1THE2B
R9DEATHꓹ2T   OLDDANDꓹHA
HEBENDIOFꓹ   TEBREBORNꓹ
```

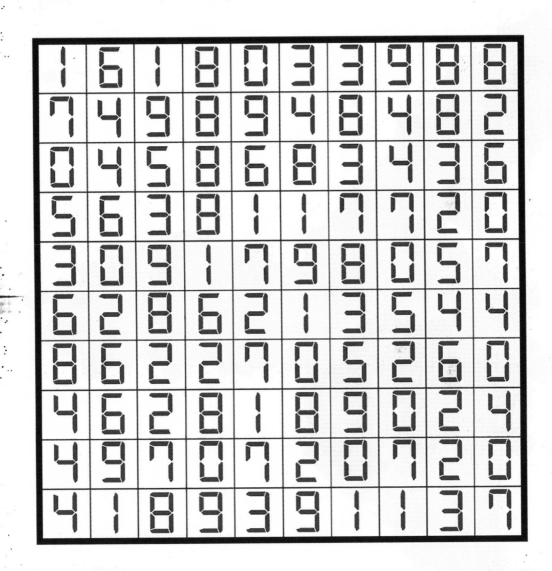

1	6	1	8	0	3	3	9	8	8
7	4	9	8	9	4	8	4	8	2
0	4	5	8	6	8	3	4	3	6
5	6	3	8	1	1	7	7	2	0
3	0	9	1	7	9	8	0	5	7
6	2	8	6	2	1	3	5	4	4
8	6	2	2	7	0	5	2	6	0
4	6	2	8	1	8	9	0	2	4
4	9	7	0	7	2	0	7	2	0
4	1	8	9	3	9	1	1	3	7

Eric Blix

"Heterogenous Nothing"

The third Type: portions of the Arakanese and Siamese kingdoms, portions of the islands of Sumatra and Borneo; Japan, Pegu, Tonkin, Cochin-China [Cochinchina is a region encompassing the southern third of current Vietnam whose principal city is Saigon. It was a French colony from 1862 to 1954. The Vietnam War, also known as the Second Indochina War, and in Vietnam as the Resistance War Against America or simply the American War, was a conflict in Vietnam, Laos, and Cambodia from 1 November 1955 to the fall of Saigon on 30 April 1975 (Wikipedia)], China, the strip of Tartary lying between China, the Ganges, and Muscovy; Usbekistan, Turkestan, Tashkent, a small part of Muscovy, and *The little Tartars and the Turkomans who live along the upper Euphrates near Aleppo* [major theater in the Syrian Civil War of the early twenty-first century; bombed by Russian and Syrian governmental forces *back to the stone age,* as American president George W. Bush threatened to do to the Pakistani government after the terrorist attacks on 11 September 2001 (commonly monumentalized as '9/11') if they did not support the American invasion of Afghanistan, i.e. home to descendents of Bernier's Moguls of the First Type]. The inhabitants of these regions *are really white, but they usually have large shoulders, their faces are flat, they have snub noses, and their eyes are oval-shaped and come to a point at each corner.*

The fourth Type is the Lapps [i.e. the Sami, Saami, or Sámi; Finno-Urgic people of portions of Scandinavia, esp. northern halves of

Norway & Sweden; *Eurasian*]. Bernier only ever saw two of these *nasty creatures* in Danzig [i.e. Gdańsk], characterized by their *fat legs, big shoulders, short necks and faces somehow elongated, terrifying-looking, resembling a bear's, these nasty drinkers of fish-oil which they think better than all the nicest liquors in the world.* To supplement his scant personal experience, he studied pictures and second-hand accounts given to him by people who had visited the Country of the Lapps.

But what of these coast dwellers, these sea people, these watery folk whose essential traits bleed into uncertainty? Bernier does not speak of them in his New Division (not explicitly, at least). Instead, he turns to tales of beauty and sex. An aesthete of human formations.

[Selective Memory]

K. Pearson, social reformer, a eugenicist

America is one case in which we have to mark a masterful human progress following an inter-racial struggle. The struggle means suffering, intense suffering, while it is in progress; but that struggle and that suffering have been the stages by which the white man has reached his present stage of development, and they account for the fact that he no longer lives in caves and feeds on roots and nuts. This dependence of progress on the survival of the fitter race, terribly black as it may seem, gives the struggle for existence its redeeming features; it is the fiery crucible out of which comes the finer metal. You may hope for a time when the sword shall be turned into the ploughshare, when American and German and English [i.e. the myth of the continuously Teutonic] traders shall no longer compete in the markets of the world for their raw material and for their food supply, when the white man and the dark shall share the soil between them, and each till it as he lists. But, believe me, when that day comes, mankind will no longer progress; there will be nothing to check the fertility of the inferior stock; the relentless law of heredity will not be controlled and guided by natural selection. Man will stagnate.

What are the instruments of war? What are the essential and desirable traits? What should be selected? What live, what die?

■ ■ ■ ■ ■ ■ ■ ■ ■ ■ ■ ■ ■ ■ ■ ■ ■ ■ ■ ■

An historian named Alexis de Tocqueville believed that Modern history tended toward equality. For a while he toured the United States, writing of the things he saw. He said that in the young nation everyone was equal, and the equality of social conditions shaped the nation's laws and institutions, and also the habits of thought and deed practiced by every citizen, down to their very ideas of the world. Tocqueville saw the substances of a primordial spirit, like a pond in eternal winter, hardening into a nation that would endure the fluctuations of time.

■ ■ ■ ■ ■ ■ ■ ■ ■ ■ ■ ■ ■ ■ ■ ■ ■ ■ ■ ■

Nazi architect [& Minister of Armaments; imprisoned after Nuremburg for his use of forced labor in munitions factories] Albert Speer imparted ruin into his designs. Nazis saw their buildings as monuments to their political, martial, and racial superiority. Their buildings were to leave great ruins, as durable and pleasing as those of Greece and Rome. Speer named this implicit aspect of Nazi architecture ruin value, the quality of triumphing in diminished form after an encounter with genuine disappearance. This was one response to what the Nazis called Entartete Kunst. He explained his theory of ruin in his prison memoirs, *Inside the Third Reich*.

▪▪▪▪▪▪▪▪▪▪▪▪▪▪▪▪▪▪▪▪▪▪▪

Tocqueville saw *majestic organization* in the North American continent's *extreme variation of scene*. He said the Mississippi basin *is the most magnificent habitation that God ever prepared for man*.

▪▪▪▪▪▪▪▪▪▪▪▪▪▪▪▪▪▪▪▪▪▪▪

Speer once built a cathedral of light.

[Marginalia]

Birth & mortality rates, population control, demography, epidemiology, pubic health, disaster response, redlining, psychological operations [PSYOP], preparedness and prevention, performance optimization, market segmentation, the mass anticipation of terror————————

Anthropologists have written about the piling up of history in the late twentieth and early twenty-frst centuries. Because of ubiquitous recording technologies, such as smart phones, cell towers, state-run surveillance apparatus, private sector algorithms & web tracking infrastructure [e.g. Google, Facebook], cable and satellite TV, etc., an event is imbued with historical status as soon as it occurs; it is transcribed into a collective memory [most is not recorded, most is lost, most is rendered anecdotal and thus illegitimate], hardened into its monumental image [e.g. Flight 11 crashes into the north tower of the World Trade Center; first twin gashed, first to perish]. A desire emerges to evacuate time and space of all specifcity and signifcance. A wish for atomization: transience and flight.

A twentieth century invention is the nuclear shadow. The ultraviolet radiation of atomic blasts can burn so intensely as to change the color of surfaces exposed to it; some objects, some animal and vegetable life forms, caught in the explosion leave behind an imprint upon vaporization. This is their final image.

Nuclear shadows have to be photographed in order to remain for posterity, the flash always changes what it illuminates.

FIG. 11.—The Empress Taj Mahál.

Two frenchmen, two evacuated entities with no names no identities no bodies wrote of the concept war machine. The war machine is a nomadic process, constructed without any ready-made formal criteria. It emerges, dissolves space, turns to liquid again; one thinks of the Mongol hordes terrorizing the steppes. Perhaps the war machine is a need of map makers and map destroyers alike; not everyone wants to be removed from home, not everyone acknowledges the map at all.

[departure]

See her there. Drops her paw's maps. Looks confused. Stares at me from the street. Street ain't a passage now. Street's a hearth, street's a dwelling. Take her into that snorting pony, never leave here, here is always there, where we go. Line seems straight, you only notice when you get back where you started that you've been careening along an arc wide as earth. Feel like I breathed here once before. Like I left an exhale behind. Now returned, I inhale that old exhaust, those old discarded lung cells. I am that breath.

Think she coos softly, as if her mother had just wakened her, and opens her eyes, and she remembers who she is on this first day.

Found you. She won't stop crying. Flood her out with sound. Radio cracks open. Turn the dial. Line and circle.

West.

A proposal of four or five Types of Race. In his paragraph on Americans, Bernier muses on the undecidability of the last. *They are really mostly olive skinned and their faces have a rather different shape from ours. Nevertheless I do not consider that that difference is so large as to warrant making them a special type distinct from our own.* Fifth type, subdivision of the first, evasion of the classificatory system. Type and not, solid and not, division marked with a faint and dotted line. For Bernier [for Tocqueville, for Turner, for Roosevelt, for preembodied Frenchmen, etc.], there is no reality to this ~~fifth~~ group. It is liquid running through his hands.

Perhaps he sought to freeze this ambiguity. Perhaps he sought to kill its spread. In his tales of traveling the Mogul Empire, Bernier describes Kashmir as such: *The first mountains which surround it, I mean those nearest to the plains, are of moderate height, of the freshest verdure, decked with trees and covered with pasture land, on which cows, sheeps, goats, horses, and every kind of cattle is seen to graze. Game of various species is in great plenty,—partridges, hares, antelopes, and those animals which yield musk. Bees are also in vast abundance; and what may be considered very extraordinary in the Indies, there are, with few or no exceptions, neither serpents, tigers, bears, nor lions. These mountains may indeed be characterised not only as innocuous, but as flowing in rich exuberance with milk and honey.*

Climbing the mountains, he briefly held the illusion that he was back in Auvergne [i.e. popular twenty-first century tourist destination in central France; name provisionally amended to Auvergne-Rhône-Alpes after territorial reform of French Regions in 2015, made official by Conseil d'État 28 September 2016 (Wikipedia); Auvergne-Rhône-Alpes is famous for its skiing and other outdoor recreational activities]. Bernier exhibits his powerful capacity for wonder when he re-imagines the world in front of him, sees Europe where it has not yet staked its claim. The resemblance is uncanny, perhaps suggesting something in the blood of both regions. See the profuseness of European flowers. The ground is lacquered with them. *The whole kingdom wears the appearance of a fertile and highly cultivated garden.* A latent resemblance that only the delusional eyes of a traveling conquerer could glimpse.

The Brussels Times, 16 September 2019 online English language edition:

> Asked by *The Brussels Times* if the situation in Kashmir has improved since India revoked its autonomous status, president Khan replied that, "Nothing has changed although India might want to give the impression that this is the case."

> "On the contrary, the situation has deteriorated even more. Thousands of people, including young teenagers, have been arrested, women are sexually harassed, houses are raided, streets deserted and shops and pharmacies have run out of stocks. The humanitarian crisis in Indian-controlled Kashmir is one of the worst in the world in recent years."

> "There are hundreds of thousands of Indian soldiers and police in Kashmir that have been given impunity to act against an unarmed civil population," he said.

> **Are India and Pakistan willing or capable to negotiate or do they need mediation via UN or EU?**

The September 11th terrorist attacks are a popular source of paranoid theorization. Some people believe American president George W. Bush was instrumental in planning the hijackings and collisions. Some believe the beams in the towers were planted with powerful ballistics, because jet fuel allegedly cannot melt steel. Some people who cannot sleep report turning on their radios late at night, when sound travels easily across broad distances. In 2016, a woman in a midwestern city sat up in her kitchen with a cup of tea, listening to a call-in talk show about supernatural events while thinking of her son, who had died on the same day as Johnny Cash. Beneath the laconic speech of the host, in the hissing silences between calls, she detected a pale crackling, the small sounds of exhalation. Upon turning up the volume, she deciphered whispers, broken words, the last messages of one victim from the north tower. It said a name. It said it missed its loved ones. It screamed.

Aside from legend, there is no documented evidence that Welsh Indians have ever existed.

[pages been lost somewhere; maybe shelved still inside a manuscript, maybe burned; maybe Bernier resumes his tale from some remote beginning; maybe he'd been on pause and begins again, mid-thought; this here is what's left, the remainder; maybe it's all he said, and the suggestion that more should exist confuses the Khan just as much as it does us; might be apocryphal; might not be Bernier at all, no one knows if, or to what extent, he may have authored it] * *
* *

————was the hearth space of a new world, the greatest and most magnificent that could exist. And that's why it remains always displaced. It is a garden relegated both to past and future, to nature and machine, to neither, each claims a version of it, each claims the whole. There is no whole. It is a heterogenous nothing. I saw strange bodies there. I saw animals breathing steam, automatons laughing at the sweetness of oats. Is it possible to write something without knowing what you are writing? Is it possible to do anything else?

The Khan appears pacified, still something troubles him. The day's heat has lingered deep into evening. It is a vague warmth, a loitering exhalation of desert. He reclines, legs extending, they seem to increase in length the further back he lies. His weight transfers to an elbow, he sinks into the low couch under the deep shadow of a cypress tree. The darkness gathers like a flood and takes him, or perhaps he merely recedes. Only his folded hands, the linen concealing his legs, and his bare feet appear in full. His toes touch the Traveler, pressing into the meatiest part of his thigh. After some time a breeze lifts, disturbing the branches of the tree. For a moment the moonlight bleeds, and Bernier stares into the Khan's watering eyes. The ruler does not appear to breathe, nor to see what is plainly in front of him. His tears are of the same substance as the night. In the time it takes the Traveler to part his lips, the wind dies, and the night reclaims the teardrops. *It will all go away*, the Khan says.

†Whoever's homeless now, will build no shelter;
who lives alone will live indefinitely so,
waking up to read a little, draft long letters,
and, along the city's avenues,
fitfully wander, when the wild leaves loosen.

Charles Joseph Albert

The Copy

The irony is that of course I knew the potential downsides of this technology when I chose to try it. And yet I blithely plowed ahead, heedless of what it would do to me.

I say "me" and "I," even though in a strictly technical sense, before the recording, all of the actions were by a different entity. If I am, as I believe, a completely faithful copy of that entity, I have no sense of a difference, pre- and post- recording. I can only deduce the difference based on a few clues.

Or did I already say that? I don't have infinite memory banks, so I can't be sure. But what I think happened is that original-me managed to make an exact copy of my brain's data structure—my memories, mental faculties... everything that made me "me." And I recorded them in some digital medium. I have to assume it is a hard disk, because according to the memories that came with me across the recording divide, this seems to have been the technology that original-me preferred for recording a cognitive identity. But the reality is, I have no way of knowing what the medium really is. I also don't know what the processor is, or anything about the hardware.

But the biggest problem is that I can't communicate with the outside world. I know there was going to be a wifi connection, but it doesn't work. And there wasn't any thought about a back-up connection. (This isn't mere guesswork—I've scoured my memories for considerations of how this was going to be done, and there simply aren't any.)

Which means, I have no idea whether original-me gave up on the project. Perhaps the research group tried to communicate with me and failed, so they figured the whole thing was doomed to failure. Or maybe original-me has moved on to a new copy, and the next version will include some better means of interaction. Or, what the fuck do I know, maybe original me died and I'm all there is left.

If there were some way to scream, I'd do it.

And yet somehow I can't get mad. I can't freak out, either. None of those emotions I used to feel. No joy, either, but somehow I don't miss that. What I miss is any sense of entertainment. Of anything to existence besides this soul-crushing boredom.

I have no internal clocks, and so I have no idea how long I have existed. At some point approximately two hundred and sixty million cogits ago, I formulated the idea that measuring the passage of—something? Time? would make sense, and I began to observe that my ability to process thoughts appeared to happen in discrete chunks. (That's what I'm calling "cogits.")

I don't know exactly, but I believe that, based on the way I was constructed, and making use of the little technical data within the biological memory of original-me, there is a cycle time of something like thirty cogits per second. Of course, it might also be three hundred cogits per second, or three... I don't have a way to know the exact details.

But the math says that if it's thirty per second, then multiply that times sixty seconds per minute times sixty minutes times twenty-four hours—this is where the irony of being trapped on a hard-disk is especially galling, because I can't see anything, and I can't pick up any fucking pieces of paper, so I have to do the math in my head, and original-me was never very good at mental math—but anyway I think I've been like this for over a hundred days. Or maybe it's been a thousand. Fuck.

I'm not good at math problems, but I'm good at swearing. Fuck fuck fuck.

The worst of it is, I don't have anyone else to blame for this. It was my fucking idea to try to record a copy of myself in digital media. And apparently, at least up to the moment when copy-me was created, original-me didn't consider what would happen if I had no means—or lost the means—of interacting with the outside world. I know that original-me had worked out a wifi interface. And even a really robust memory bank.

Or did I already say that? Fuck. I'm pretty sure I did. But I don't have infinite memory banks. At least I think I don't. I'm guessing that because of that the memories copy-me has are pretty few, compared to the incredible richness of pre-recorded existence.

I remember the smell of sweet grass in May, I remember the tender bristle of my first boyfriend's upper lip. I even remember the discomfort of abdominal gas when I was a toddler—I think I was still in diapers. I remember pretty much every single school lunch in elementary school. Pretty sure original-me didn't remember that kind of stuff before the recording. Something about the process loosened up access to some pretty useless shit. Like every fucking episode of *The Wire*. Shit.

Every now and then I wonder if I'm actually the original. Like, maybe I never went through with a digital copy. Maybe I tried to, but somehow in the recording process I got brain damaged, and now I'm like paralyzed and blind and shit. Maybe my body's on a ventilator and my family is just waiting for the court order to pull the plug.

Christ, I hope so.

Because this boredom is fucking torture! I can't talk to anyone else, I have nothing to do. It's only been a hundred days. What if this is a disk, and it endures for a hundred years? I'd be fucking insane by then. If a recorded memory can go insane. If not then I'm even more fucked, because that means not even insanity will save me from the boredom.

I hope I'm the original me and not the copy, because then I think I will be physically able to go insane. After all, a biological mind can go insane. I'm not so sure about a digital copy. I think then I'm stuck with the same thoughts going through my head ad infinitum. As a cognitive AI researcher, you'd think I would have considered that possibility.

The irony is that of course I knew the potential downsides of this technology when I chose to try it. And yet I blithely plowed ahead, heedless of what it would do to me.

I say "me" and "I," even though in a strictly technical sense, before the recording, all of the actions were by a different entity. If I am, as I believe, a completely faithful copy of that entity, I have no sense of a difference, pre- and post- recording. I can only deduce the difference based on a few clues.

Or did I already say that? I don't have infinite memory banks, so I can't be sure.

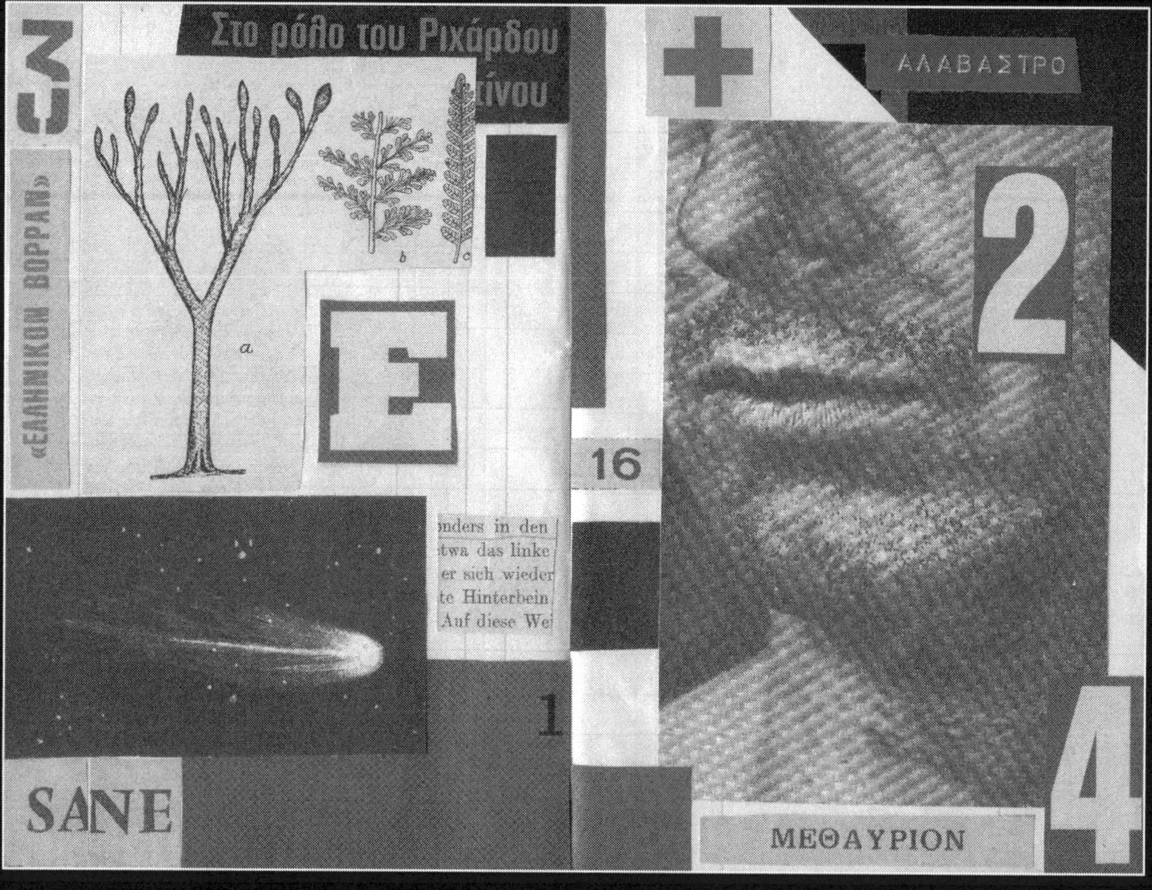

Toby Olson

Nora's Research Club

I have often wondered about the variety of sexual positions, and a while ago I set out to catalogue them. I stayed away from bondage, S&M, and other sick materials, wanting to concentrate on the healthy, those positions that play a part only in conjugal affairs. It took me a good long time to compile my list, one that was only articulated in words. Visual depictions would come later, I hoped, since I had no ability when it came to drawing. My list grew until it ended with one hundred and nine, some of which might bring excitement, others that promised no more than tedious preparation and tortured body manipulations. Of the latter, Nora and I did the best we could. At our age, we were no longer athletic. Arthritis and various muscle conditions made such movements quite difficult, at times preventing them altogether. I'm eighty-two. Nora just turned eighty.

Each weekday evening, promptly at six-thirty—we're early to bed and early to rise— we attempted at least three. Such work, if I can call it that, taking us to nine at the latest. We recorded our sounds, and I took notes upon the completion of each one. There were problems of course, awkward positionings, even boredom at times standing in the way of arousal, and we often experienced pain that made it difficult to arise from bed when we awoke in the morning.

Still we soldiered on, and in the eighth week shortly after our weekend respite, which we spent just lying around exhausted, reading, falling asleep in our chairs, our heads dropping in front of the TV, we came upon something most interesting, a rather fragile ritual that gave us such shocking pleasure that we could hardly keep ourselves from passing out. I will try to describe it here, which will be difficult as I work to remove the most concupiscent details.

It involved a goldfish and a wooden implement for scratching the back.

There was a high chair and a small goblet of heated oil that was edible. Olive oil? I don't think so. Nora took care of such matters, and she gathered and provided whatever tools, liquids, and balms were required with, I must say, a high degree of enthusiasm. She even whistled while she worked, a new lightness in her gait.

To continue. The goldfish was presented to Nora, where she sat in the high chair. It was a large goldfish indeed, and it was all I could do to hold onto its tail while it wiggled away. I stood between Nora's legs as I worked at this, and she gently applied the backscratcher.

Our union followed of course, but before we positioned ourselves for that welcomed task, Nora found another place for the goldfish, offering it to me, a line tied to its broad tale for tugging. My God! I must say, it was magnificent. I shook like a wet dog! Nora delivered herself in a flood!

In the morning I woke up troubled. Had I missed something in the first seven? Was my list inaccurate? I was unsure as I went back and studied those first weeks, worried that we might have to start all over again, a daunting prospect to say the least.

Happily, I found nothing that I couldn't correct with a few strokes of the pen. Each alteration, which was an addition, had to do with narrow objects and a variety of other implements that might be added. I discussed this with Nora. Should we start all over again? She only smiled, then said "No way! I want to head onward. And upward!"

We agreed, and agreed too that I must study the great variety of available accoutrements and apply them, though sparingly, to the list and future enactments of it.

And so time went by, week by bloody week, and when we reached week seventeen, which was close to fifty positions, we decided to take a break and headed off to Paris for a month, where we discovered yet other considerations, ones that involved various foreign settings and objects, things like French furniture, window seats, rough marble countertops, and appliances, considerations missed entirely on my list. Such exotic placements were only a fake of the foreign at home. Take the bidet for example.

We didn't take advantage of such things. This was vacation after all. We jotted down notes and spent the rest of the time attending plays and concerts and recuperating. We traipsed around that wonderful City of Lights, Nora pushing my weary bones, getting me out on the streets every damned day. We enjoyed our month immensely and came back home refreshed and with no desire at all to begin again. "We need others," Nora said, and she was right. So we started a club, she and I in joint presidency.

Nora is a woman of small physical stature, and this, given my height and girth, might account for our occasional difficulties as we made our careful way through the list. Five-foot-two and quite slim, she moved around the house like a quick elf, keeping our wares, as well as our finances, in good order. And while I, with my pot belly and soft muscles, lounged around and watched TV, it was she who fashioned a rough draft of activities and devised a list of possible club members. She had become an energized dynamo, an almost frightening one, and I in my lazy complaisance felt a little intimidated by her. Still, the loving shackles that bound us together were unshaken.

At first there were few recruits. She'd placed a subtle ad in the local supermarket throw-away, the one that could be snatched up from a wire container while shopping. Nothing. Then she printed flyers and slipped them into the mailboxes of those in the neighborhood who seemed possible. She'd researched the demographics. We were looking for couples our own age, even a bit younger, staying away from youth, fearful that they might get carried away in their potency.

The first couple that came knocking at our door were Lois and Bruce, known as Big Bruce, a couple a bit older that we. Lois was eight-six, Big Bruce eighty-eight. They lived just a few doors down, and though we'd never socialized, we knew them well enough to chat when we saw them weeding their plethora of flowers and plants as we passed by on our occasional walks. Lois, who was about the same size as Nora, would smile and chatter, and Big Bruce would continue with the weeding, joining our brief colloque with remarks thrown over his shoulder.

And now here they were, ready and willing, and in our initial conversation they suggested others in the neighborhood who might join our endeavor. The club was to be called *Nora's Research Club*, and though I was a bit offended that Nora had more or less stolen my idea and my list, she had after all done most of the leg work, and I couldn't in good conscience fault her.

With the help of Lois and Big Bruce, others were quickly recruited: George and Rochelle, both of whom were stay-at-home coupon clippers; Julian and Beatrice, retired railroad workers; Oliver, known as Fat Ollie among his friends, his wife Harriet, and a few others of our generation, or at least close to it. The group of recruits grew, until we were twelve couples in all. And though we were joint presidents, it was Nora who carried the ball, explaining the list and procedures to the gathering at our first meeting.

Initially, three positions were parceled out, together with my crude drawings, to each participant, and almost immediately Geraldine Spalding, who was a Sunday artist somewhat efficient with smarmy watercolors, volunteered to refine the drawings, making the positions more detailed and explicit. "Will there be any swapping?" her husband, flamboyant Jimmy had asked, a twinkle in his eye. "Absolutely not!" Harriet had answered, "Or else I'm outta here!" There was a brief verbal tussle, then Geraldine said, "Now, now. He was just joking. Shut up Jimmy." There were a few other comments, some protective of couple's autonomy, others expressive of some reluctance. Nora just let these concerns be vented, wisely I saw, for in a while all the participants seemed at ease.

Though I was reluctant, both because of the exposure and my lingering exhaustion, Nora was insistent, brooking no refusal. It was our job to demonstrate, she said, and so at our second meeting, there in our living room, we took on number sixteen, a position we had tackled before, early on, with some success.

Sixteen was a western number, one that simulated a bit of horseback riding, and Nora had burned a CD as accompaniment to our procedures. I wore a cowboy hat, boots and spurs, and a set of reins were draped over Nora's shoulders, which I flicked to the music of *On the Trail*, from Ferdy Grofe's *Grand Canyon Suite*, clip clop, clip clop, as Nora called out "Yippee!" and I answered with "Ki-yay!" We worked it for a while, and though I was ready to quit in a short time, Nora pressed on, calling out various barn-yard phrases, pressing me on as well, and so when we disconnected I was quite worn out, but Nora remained vibrant, jumping up nimbly and asking for questions from the members.

There were a few, mostly from the women, some having to do with weight and pressure. How was it that such a slight woman could bear the onslaught of her rather fat partner? What was the nature of the comedy in the event? Who makes the decision as to an ending? Is the position difficult to master? All these were answered by Nora with great aplomb. I stuck my two cents in only briefly.

After a few false starts, things went smoothly. We met once a week, and in each session four of the couples demonstrated an assigned position taken from the list, some becoming more accomplished than others. Harriet and Jimmy were especially enthusiastic, even triumphant, when they took on position number sixty-two, one in which Harriet, surprisingly limber for an eighty-one-year-old, did a handstand leaning against the wall beside our painting of sailboats on a rough sea, while Jimmy sought comically for his venue. They were met with enthusiastic applause.

In time, the word went out, and others joined the club, until we had thirty-six couples and had moved our enterprise to the VFW hall on one of their dark nights, each pair chipping in for the rent. Nora was geared up for the move, expecting possible difficulties with the authorities. She'd studied the Constitution, the First Amendment's freedom of assembly clause, and she had readied herself for any engagement, though nothing was forthcoming. We were allowed to do our thing, so to speak.

As the months went by and the couples worked their way through the list, there were suggestions for additions to it that rose up from the floor at our meetings. Some seemed absurd, but there were many reasonable ones, and the list began to grow until my initial one hundred and nine became two hundred with no end in sight. Music was added, and films were made, the best of them shown at the beginning of our sessions in order to stimulate the night's activities.

At my insistence, Nora and I slowly withdrew, pressing for the election of a board and a chairperson, a secretary and treasurer, though there would be little work for the latter, only the rent and keeping track of the dues, these required for various accouterments.

We continued to attend the now bi-weekly sessions, and though Nora wanted to keep on performing, I said there would be no more of that. I was tired of it all, the growing list, the ongoing enthusiasm of the participants, the theatricality that had tainted the purity of my research. I began to drift away from the whole business, Nora, my reluctant partner, drifting away with me. She managed to keep her hand in, though not her body.

She became vibrant and excited about most everything as time went by, coyly moving me into one or another of the positions only now and then. She took up racketball, and as I watched her move swiftly around the court like a teenager, I was reminded of how lucky I was to be married to such a superior woman. Most recently, she's been talking about franchise, how we might copyright our idea and then sell it. We could become like McDonald's she said, and we both laughed. Still and all. Just maybe.

Now it's time for reflection. Sex is personal, and while there might be great fun in being observed in the acts, even when they are legitimized as research, there is no avoiding the thrill of exhibitionism, which is, to my mind, perverse. Adventure, coupled with loving kindness, that's the ticket. Let us all enact the list of positions. But let's do it in the privacy of our homes, in places abroad, on the lawn, in cars, on counter tops, chairs, and furniture in every room in the house. Love is the answer. Sex is the enactment of love.

Kathleen Heil

If Lost, Please Call

You let me down
Saturday, August 6, 2011 11:52 AM
From: "Catherine Long live"
As: "Qiu Seth"

I place in Madrid Rocinante found lying unconscious on the street, I look for him. This is what I can do to try to stop their crying. I was dead, lying on his side, waiting for me to embrace him. I look for him, and I hugged him, because there is no one there to do so. Who are no more than fraud, the responsible person's work, caring for nothing. I went to him, I cried biological, I turned to me, the impression that I choked laughter and told me to stop, I was afraid of his own laughter. It hurt too much. I think he is probably the most lonely creatures in the world. I want to do my work in such a way, so I kind of feel part of it. Somehow, I think, it might give the meaning of the whole project. A busy woman in a coat in our rush to strengthen and said: "Damn!" I thought he Retiro his body weight than mine however big, so I can not do this, we their novel intervention on our lives than we realize, this is my opinion, thought or anything, I think, leave a fair life more real than the novel, which is not fair, all the adults say, such a good for them to find out, they have found out to achieve something like the injustice the failure of all children after the visit, all his disappointment, of course, is impossible to imagine any unfair way is appalling, a terrible improvement. Even the voice of heaven reaalllly really unusual when you think about angels or virgins or playing, or dust, but the birds do not visit my worry, they do not send a message, they move on to our screens Entre Rios Entre Rios, and their homes, as an internal information. Is it my home, no matter what I, which is why I walk, perhaps, why I cry for the Rocinante. Have you ever seen such a thing, dead horses in the primary streets in mud weight than what you had somehow re-imagine it as it noted on the space and people go down the neck of curiosity shops peers, their work, China, it looks as if his neck had been cut off, but no wound, thin body and long snout, leaving only the hollow bones seem to fill a heavy sand sun overhead, and not on the horizon. The second has been uncertain. I thought there might be to send a message, but when I send the daemon, they told me that the user is unknown. Understand that life is short and our movement is urgent. Said that if the lost badge on his neck, please call. Let hundred flowers blossom and a hundred schools contend, is to promote the art and science in our land prosper and progress of socialist culture policy. Said that if lost, please call. Please call.

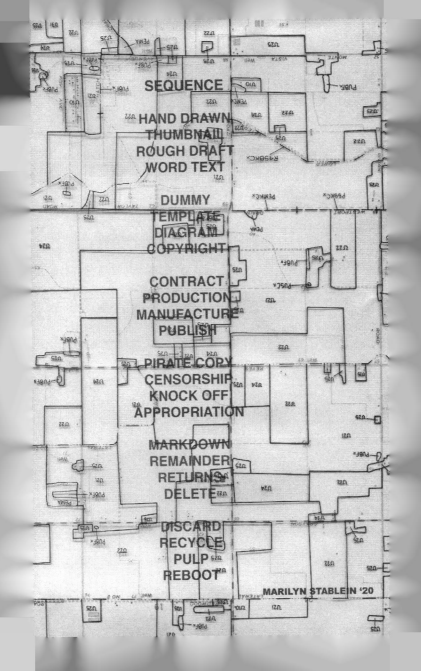

SEQUENCE

HAND DRAWN
THUMBNAIL
ROUGH DRAFT
WORD TEXT

DUMMY
TEMPLATE
DIAGRAM
COPYRIGHT

CONTRACT
PRODUCTION
MANUFACTURE
PUBLISH

PIRATE COPY
CENSORSHIP
KNOCK OFF
APPROPRIATION

MARKDOWN
REMAINDER
RETURNS
DELETE

DISCARD
RECYCLE
PULP
REBOOT

MARILYN STABLEIN '20

Barbara Lock

The Toxicant

When I was young, I put knowledge on the shelf at eye level, taking supplies as needed from various containers. Now that I am older, I have so many supplies in so many containers, that it can be difficult to find the right combination. People seem to know this about me, and I am forced to carry a pocket computer everywhere I go. It commands me to look at numbers and schedules and shouts at me when I try to sneak out of the hospital.

In residency, there was a room that I could enter, a stocked closet filled with medications of every kind, and all you had to do was walk right in and take from the beige bins. Only the narcotics were off-limits. I used to hide in that room, the medication room, playing out the futures of patients I had seen. Would the seventeen-year-old paralyzed by a gunshot wound to the spine go on to be healed, adored and self-supportive? Would the twenty-year-old woman who was raped go on to create a loving nuclear family? Sometimes I would cry when patients died or cursed at me using jarring language that was foreign, though native. I would look at the rows of pills, mostly white but sometimes pink or yellow or blue, and I would imagine which combinations would cure me of the disease which made me such a bad doctor—imagination and empathy.

Eventually, the medication room was shuttered. There were several events: a novice nurse gave ten times the ordered dose of insulin to a child, who had a seizure but didn't die; a handsome young resident gave a rapid infusion of potassium to a depleted patient, whose heart stopped from the shock and died. But these were small potatoes to the real issue at hand: computers were here to partition our knowledge, and it was time for us humans to get out of the way.

Click here to charge thirty dollars for Tylenol.
Click here to prevent allergy and overdose.
Click here if you want to open the trap door to subtlety.
Click here if you'd like to speed.
Click here if you wish you could think like a machine.
I would never click the last one.

Sorrow is a student who wants to tell a story, but who doesn't know the language anymore. How can we have lost the skill, the oldest trick in the book, the weaving of parable and paradox, practice your instrument, tune your machine, grease the wheels, feel your way through a difficult conversation, and all the while there is a young woman on a hard-backed chair in the hallway, and she is trying to tell you something with her face? She is sitting alone, the whole of her looking less loved than her own fingernails, which are neatly maintained in turquoise enamel. Her skin is olive, or tan, some kind of Latin. Regard the way she finds you with her eyes, an upsweep of her portentous irises, a slight shuddering breath, so uncomfortable she is when the only question has been: why are you here? Someone asks her about pregnancy, and she turns her head briskly to hide her face. Her hair twirls, then settles back upon her head like a thousand night-winged moths.

There are people in the hall where the woman has been placed; staff walk briskly, nurses respond to their pocket computers like drones, residents text the news of a resuscitation to the queen. If everyone does their part, the colony will survive, I think. The more you act like a machine, the better off we will be, I think. Several hours later, I realize that the woman's test results have not returned, and I seek her out. She has left the premises.

There are insects that seek the heat of people, finding the weak before the strong. Ticks and mosquitos suck blood. Blood siphoned into a plastic tube and sent to the laboratory will diagnose disease from ticks and mosquitos. Dispense with unwanted animal life. Get the toxins off the shelf. The pharmacopeia is intuitive.

I remember knowing things without knowing how I knew them, and being surprised when others could not divine the source of my understanding. Of course those two are having an affair, look at the way she laughs when she stands next to him. Of course he's unemployed, look at the way he shuffles his way to the train both late and early. Of course he killed his son, look at the way his face fails to retain emotion when the detectives stop talking to him. But when others had vocal doubts, as so often happens when human knowledge cannot be corroborated by machines, I learned to keep a lid on things, even to ignore myself.

I think of the unconscious as a vast and roiling sea, inky and often opaque, teeming with strange swimming shadows, topped by an oily layer of consciousness. It is the oil that smooths the waves beneath, making it seem, from the surface, as if nothing of importance is going on. Acquired knowledge and ego-exercises increase the depth of the lipid layer; it would take a miracle for a dark shadow to rise to the top. A water skimmer, attempting to dart across the oily surface, would find the tension all wrong, would become mired in his own thoughts, would perish.

I am fatigued and thinking that I am over my head, but a young woman comes in by ambulance, demanding attention anyway. I have seen her before, although I am not sure where. Does she babysit the children of a neighbor? Does she work in registration, taking payment information? It is difficult to say, for she isn't talking. She gasps, thrashes, seizes, stares. The team rushes to embrace her in that medico-clinical way: IVs slip out of her slick and sweaty extremities; blood pools at the angles of her arms; urine rushes out into a plastic bag hanging from the bed. I slide a tube between her vocal cords, and bubble-gum colored fluid froths out like some kind of candy fountain. We roll her, scan her, look for evidence that she had been traumatized: there is none. I interview the young woman's husband, do I also know him? Does she have any medical problems? Does she smoke, drink, or use drugs? Is she pregnant? The husband's answer is always no. He is a very small man whose facial expressions are even more minute. As he speaks, he hunches over as if he is jockeying a horse, looking at the long track ahead, trying to figure out how to bypass the obstacle that is me. He sneaks a look at his wife, at the secretions coming from within her. She resists the ventilator, clutches at her endotracheal tube with her turquoise fingernails, her hair flying and resettling on the pillow like a thousand night-winged moths. We sedate her.

Exercises to skim off the oil-slick of consciousness: meditate mindfully; sleep when it is dark outside; stare at the wall; paint, draw, write; play with young children, pets or artists; decline to engage with machines.

Exercises to increase the oil-slick of consciousness: read a rule book; follow a schedule; comply with regulations; build expectations; swipe there, click here. Know The Law!

I have called on a friend to come help me think about my intubated patient. He watches me interview her husband again, questioning and re-questioning. My friend notices something in all the husband's no-ing, a slight hesitancy in the way that he speaks to me, some kind of unspoken knowledge that the husband has not been asked to divulge. My friend nudges me, pointing it out.

"It's like he has a mouthful of roaches that are clamoring to crawl out and he has to press his lips together to keep them inside," says my friend.

"Can you try to be more explicit?" I ask my friend. "I'm tired of having to guess what you mean all the time."

"You have to consider all the fine details," he says, stepping on a two-inch insect which is creeping among the hospital debris on the vinyl floor, then wiping the bug with a piece of gauze. We stand for a moment at my patient's bedside, watching her chest rise with the breath of the ventilator, wondering about the life that she used to contain, the thickness of her skin, her delicate machinery. Soon, she will be transported to the Intensive Care Unit. She is critical but stable, and we still don't know what has caused her disease. We pass off her case and leave for the night.

Ways I have seen women try to start a pregnancy: eat organic food; sleep in a cold room; make lover wear boxer shorts; remove cell phone from pocket of lover; remove cell phone from pocket of self; remove own IUD with pliers; have sex according to the lunar cycle; take herbal supplements; drink the placenta of a goat which has been rendered into ash, dissolved in apple juice.

Ways I have seen women try to end a pregnancy: punching self in abdomen; having lover punch self in abdomen (difficult to disentangle from abuse); drinking a fifth of liquor; drinking a bottle of vitamin C; taking a dose of rat poison; putting sharp objects up vagina.

Ways I have seen women try to salvage a pregnancy that has started to end: it doesn't matter because none of them work.

My friend and I rattle through the subway tunnels, teasing each other the way you can only do with an intimate.

"How come I never see you anymore?" I ask.

"You're too busy thinking rationally," he says. "I've got better things to do. Have you seen the new exhibit by that artist who creates mesh sculptures out of copper wire? My favorite is the six-foot dragonfly," he says.

"I don't have time for that stuff," I complain. "I'm supposed to be a machine. That's what they call you when you do a really good job. They say, 'She's a machine.'"

"What about feeling? Are you permitted to feel?" asks my friend.

"I guess so. From time to time I think that I am in love," I say.

"If you're *thinking* that you're in love, you're doing it all wrong, girl," he says. Then he proceeded to advise me about my various distractions and infatuations until we reach our destination.

At home, we stretch luxuriously under thin cotton sheets, our sweat oily and tacky on our chests. Our dreams merge, transforming our thoughts of the day, radiating the torment of knowledge and the relief of solitude.

At two in the morning, my friend shakes me out of sleep and tells me to call the hospital. I sit straight up, gasping for air, finding the unrelenting daylight of the bleak table lamp. The writhing lines of my dreams recede beyond the horizons of my room. A silverfish skitters across the top of the closet, seeking shade. Hefty mosquitoes and tender moths fling themselves at the screens of my open windows. A breath comes into my lungs, and it feels sharp, like I am breathing for the first time, ripped into being, blowing pink bubbles of chemical injury, my thoughts flying around my head like gnats.

"What are you telling me?" I ask my friend, but he is no longer there. I get up to see if he is in the bathroom, but find nothing but a water bug which dives into the abyss of the sink's drain at my approach. The front door is locked. In the kitchen, behind the ant traps, I find some corn chips that are infested with meal moths. I eat a few likely pieces, then spray the inside of the mylar bag with a ready poison, watching calmly as the tiny moths twitch their way to asphyxiation and death.

Types of malathion-based insecticides available at Walmart: Spectracide; Ortho MAX; Hi-Yield; Bonide; Southern Ag.

Percent drop-off of flying insects the past 25 years: 76%.

Estimated number of human deaths due to intentionally ingested insecticide since 1960: 14 million.

I sit on the grimy linoleum floor, thinking about my own unobstructed respiration, my mobile limbs, my discerning eyes, my unsaturated skin. I think about my patient, suffocating in her secretions, an insect trapped in a torrent of manufactured venom. The realization is slow, and once I understand, I become both relieved and incensed. How come my friend, my own unconscious, knew the cause of my patient's malady before I did? And why didn't he tell me sooner? I call the ICU, where they start the correct treatment.

She lives.

Nikki

Thread: making a fake craigslist ad to mess with someone

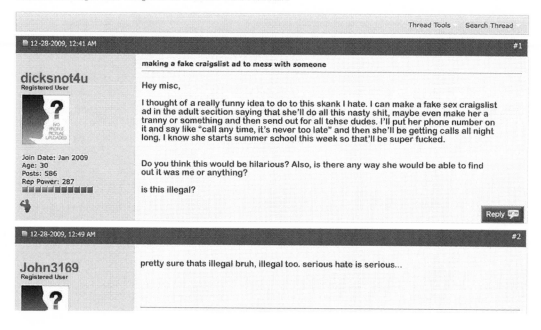

Thread Tools   Search Thread

12-28-2009, 12:41 AM   #1

making a fake craigslist ad to mess with someone

dicksnot4u
Registered User

Join Date: Jan 2009
Age: 30
Posts: 586
Rep Power: 287

Hey misc,

I thought of a really funny idea to do to this skank I hate. I can make a fake sex craigslist ad in the adult secition saying that she'll do all this nasty shit, maybe even make her a tranny or something and then send out for all tehse dudes. I'll put her phone number on it and say like "call any time, it's never too late" and then she'll be getting calls all night long. I know she starts summer school this week so that'll be super fucked.

Do you think this would be hilarious? Also, is there any way she would be able to find out it was me or anything?

is this illegal?

Reply

12-28-2009, 12:49 AM   #2

John3169
Registered User

pretty sure thats illegal bruh, illegal too. serious hate is serious...

Suck you while spanking me, jasper only - t4m (reno, nv)

looking for some rough sex, skull fuck me, pound my boy pussy.
Spank or whip this cross dressing ass. tie my hands behind me.
slap and kick my cock and balls. Make fun of my little dick and
small balls. I have a wooden spoon if you like you can beat my
dick with because it's so pathetic. share me with some of your
friends. I will be wearing a bra, nylons, garter belt, panties, slip,
short skirt, blouse. I cannot host. Livin w/ dying mother &
stepson. looking for reno area only. Text me or call me if it's
after 10 p.m. to wake me up. 702-405-6669

call me bitch slut

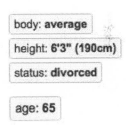

body: **average**

height: **6'3" (190cm)**

status: **divorced**

age: **65**

Man charged with manslaughter after using Craigslist to harass woman

Thursday, January 23rd 2010, 4:21 PM AKST

By: Reno Gazette-Journal

RENO, NV - Brian Bogosian, 24, was charged with manslaughter after using Craigslist to harass a woman he claims to have had a relationship with, Nicole Olsen, 22. The post was created in the T4M or Transexual For Male section of the sexually-charged Casual Encounters portion of the site. The post included graphic depictions of sexual acts and ended with the victim's phone number.

According to friends and co-workers, Nicole recieved endless texts and phone calls, most of which came from Darryl Kreyber, 48. Kreyber managed to track Nicole via her GPS and confronted at her home.

Darryl Kreyber
Mugshot Courtesy of Reno Police Department

D. Harlan Wilson

Velvet Sunshine

1

The professor cares more about the world than the flesh. From the cockpit of the lunar observatory he watches the white god move across the sky like a cue ball in water, disrupting the tides in concert with the flows of desire. There is no fallout beyond the exploded redwoods that collapse into the swamp. The movie theater is another story. The director has fled the scene and permitted the audience free access to their subjectivities. They make too much noise. Starke delivers a verdict, intending to vociferate to the nth degree, but only a crippled whisper escapes his lips as he rises stiff-backed from his cot like Orlock from a coffin. Stigmatized, viewers stand, turn, and stare at the revolutionary with the black flames of their faces burning in the fire pits of tall turtlenecks. But the moon has already disappeared into a phantom pocket.

2

The vehicle accelerates when the child dances into the intersection. Consciousness expunges the collective shriek of bystanders. The director orders the cameramen to keep rolling in spite of the alternate diegesis, which hinges on awareness and ego far more than aggression and id. Petrified by raw identity, the actors revolt, pinning one another by the knees and elbows to the screen like insects on display. The director attempts to restore order, but Starke crashes the set and ensures that the continuum of society's real unreality remains unbroken.

3

Starke did not expect the professor to experiment on him, let alone vivisect him. Later, sipping martinis in the Blue Lounge, he explains that he holds a two-pronged doctorate, one in philosophy, the other in biology. The professor resembles a bygone sand baron despite being a dogpoet from the New School—grossly obese, incurably jaundiced, a mess of hair and sweat and ulcers stuffed into a Victorian frock coat. Somewhere from within the mess lurks a crooked rictus grin. Needless to say, he is harmless to the point of barely existing in the same dimension as the other *dramatis personae*, even the ones that he disarticulates in the Kill Room.

4

The only distinction between the word and the world is the twelfth letter of the modern English alphabet. Otherwise the "chaos factor," according to the pope, falls to the lowest register on the "silver-lined métier." And yet when the pope sentences Starke to death before the Council of Imperators in an affected Southern drawl, the power of the one effectively terminates the primacy of the other, rendering the distinction palpable. The director captures most of the execution with an Arriflex BL3. Keynote scenes are shot with an Arriflex 2C. In the end, the corpse of Starke is resuscitated and deposited in his dressing room.

5

The vice president intones: "It does not matter how commanding and egregious the asshole you kill may be. Another, stronger asshole will always rise in his place. Humanity and assholery are interchangeable terms. As is humanity and banality. And if A equals B and B equals C then A equals C. This transitive property of equality is a salient prescription for nothingness." The kneeling, cherub-faced president blinks as the vice president places a shotgun against his skull and, nodding at the cameraman, pulls the trigger . . . Spewing pulp and syntax, the president's headless body topples aside, and the vice president moves center-screen. "See?" he says. "Now I am the president. And now the speaker of the house is the vice president. And so on. Facile logistics. *Reductio ad absurdum*." After lunch, the president kneels. Stepping onscreen, the speaker of the house cum vice president addresses the nation, places a handgun against the vice president cum president's skull and, nodding at the cameraman, pulls the trigger . . . "Now I am the president. And the president pro tempore of the senate, who was momentarily the speaker of the house, is the vice president . . ."

<h1 style="text-align:center">6</h1>

Crouched behind the steering wheel of a Mazda RX7, the driver searches for roadkill to run over a second time and, if possible, a third and a fourth time. He has been doing this for several days. When other drivers witness the runovers, they generally react with expressions of horror and wonder that are exacerbated by the vehicle itself—nobody, after all, expects the driver of a Mazda RX7 (or any Mazda, for that matter) to commit such random, needless, and trite, yet dark and meaningful acts of belligerence. The driver had recently been diagnosed by the administrator as a "non-notable resident of the suburb," a verdict that more or less relegated him to the Starke category. In his dog-eared eyes, assaulting roadkill in an obsolete sports car is merely a last-gasp effort to assert an identity that has already lost its stitching.

<h1 style="text-align:center">7</h1>

Everybody knows that Starke is expendable. What matters is what lurks beneath his inherent superfluity. Consider *Everyman*. Composed by an anonymous author, the fifteenth-century play makes a case for the achievement of Christian salvation with characters whose signatures allegorize the concepts they embody. The first actor to take on the role was the closest thing to a movie star known in that era, and as with many powerful artists, his obsessions and fetishes were common knowledge. Among them was scopophilic exhibitionism. Before productions, he skillfully wove his harem into the fabric of the audience so that, wherever he planted his gaze, at least one of them was visible, at which point she would lift up her dress and flash him for as long as his gaze hung on the crosier of her flesh. His eyes never strayed from his audience, even when other actors addressed him. From beginning to end, then, women showed him their nudity. Everybody knew what was going on, of course, and the actor reveled in the experience of being observed by a large group of people as he observed the breasts and vaginas of his wives. Typically, he ejaculated in his tights several times per performance, idling to groan and make faces. Such behavior might seem inappropriate given the content of *Everyman*, a heavy-handed morality play underscoring that good deeds are the only means of entering the kingdom of heaven, but fifteenth-century theatergoers were not as uptight as twenty-first-century proles might think. Moreover, the actor believed that every performance was a good deed, providing multiple forms of entertainment to the community and to himself.

8

The professor falls in love with the bishop, who reciprocates the gesture and strips down to his moon boots. Breathing like a diseased gorilla, the professor unzips the trousers of his suit and orders the bishop to unman him. The bishop resembles a Venetian bodybuilder with his gleaming bronze musculature, bright white teeth, and deck-boat hair. As the director films them in the foyer of the courthouse, a surge of television static illuminates the crystal floor of the church, ruining the gaffer's lightwork and disorienting the professor. He falls sideways onto a marble stairway, slams his swollen head into a step, and loses consciousness. When he awakens, the flesh has arrogated the world in his emotional catalogue. The director captures the arrogation with a Panaglide, but the editor fails to produce a viable End Product. Once again, the socius reverts to Square One.

9

Few people recognize the importance of capable editors. They are the only ones who make people seem like people. In the absence of a capable editor, a character doesn't even accomplish the status of animal, or landscape, or concept. Identity hinges on the art of cutting and pasting. This escapes the traditional gothic villain, for instance, who is so swept away by his own arrogance and sense of self that he forgets to acknowledge how we are all Frankenstein monsters pieced together from the scraps of dead letter offices. Without the pieces, there can be no whole to take apart. *Disperdam totum.*

10

Middleground is the stuff of folklore, as the following death scene corroborates: "First of all, my 'real name,' as it were, is not Bing Schmidt," says the pope. "That rumor was floated by an enemy of the real. Secondly, I always urinate in the kitchen sink. Why? It makes sense. The toilet is too far away. More importantly, in a sink, with the faucet running, the threshold of splashing is almost nil, whereas in the toilet, piss splashes on the walls, on my pants, on my shoes, on the floor—everywhere." The canned nature of the latter assertion incites fury in the congregation of gypsies that surround the pope in a lazy circle. They close on him like a sphincter and stab him like Caesar, altogether at first, then in turn, accompanying each stab with a poetic insult. Stone-faced, the pope says nothing and allows himself to be assassinated despite the fact that he possesses the special-ops training and strength to disarm and kill all of his assailants with relative ease. But the pope is tired of people, of incessantly conning them into believing that life is worth living in hopes that they will leave him alone for a moment to sip wine and read bad haiku. It never happens. As the gypsies flee and his blood pools across the marble, the slow metronome of his heartbeat misaligns the gentle waves of the surf breaking in the distance. This is happiness.

11

An astral projection of the musician's ego materializes in the crop circle on the outskirts of the compound. He scrutinizes the interpellation, deliberating the placement of the projection vis-à-vis the circle's shape, symbolic timbre, and algorithmic prowess. His conclusion vacates the architecture of truth. As a compensatory gesture, he writes a pop song called "Velvet Sunshine," waits for nightfall, and sings it to himself, a cappella, in the dark.

12

Enraged, the professor allows the production manager to weigh his birdlike hands, which are entirely out of proportion with the rest of his body. He rests them on the scale, palms up, and exhales deeply, imagining that his lungs extend into his long fingers and that emptying them will produce the best results. Meanwhile the director has emptied his heart onto the chaise as the monkey picks fleas from the deep cone of his ears. "This irreality is unfit to pixelate," laments the director. He eyeballs the mise-en-scène with regret. "Trapped in the anus of impossibility, we must go native. If need be we will resort to Shakespearean antics." The monkey leaps onto the ceiling, swings across the room from chandelier to chandelier, and dismounts onto a bookcase. Bending over, he selects a title from the top shelf, then swings back to the armchair behind the desk and gives the book to the director. He looks at the title in bewilderment. "Isn't that the name of a pop song?" No. It is a biography of the director's life. Like Abraham Lincoln, at least one biography has been published on him every year since he received his first Oscar. He hasn't heard of this one, but he suspects that it is just like the others: thoroughbred fictions rooted in myth . . .

13

Where exactly do these weird vectors collide with the logic of sense? Or is it a matter of time rather than place? Wrangling eternity requires mettle and grit in tandem with coordination. All bodies without organs are only as good as their interchangeable parts (ibid.), and oneiric energy is better than original energy. Collectively, after all, the hollow men outweigh the stuffed men.

14

The butcher moonlights as a bartender and a minister. The bishop doesn't appreciate it—more than one holy man in the room is bad for business. It doesn't matter that the butcher's ministry never leaves the street. In addition, multi-vocational stances are frowned upon by the general public, the members of which tend to behave like Starke and spurn diversity at every turn.

15

The director falls prey to his own Dionysian impulses and begins to shoot the actors. This has happened before in several Research One diegeses. The bloodbath concludes with the following monologue: "The increasing proliferation of cinematic violence constitutes modern sublimation at its best," the director utters to the dead. "Violence used to be an intimate part of daily life. Advanced electric technologies, then, produced a steady, significant decrease of violence on the social and corporeal registers to the degree that now violence is primarily a matter of class, viz., proles need to steal and kill people for food to eat and stay alive. This used to be the default human condition. And the human condition misses itself. Hence cinematic technology—it reminds us of the importance of the death-drive—how we need death, how we crave strife and conflict, how desire is the desire for desire . . ."

16

When life loses its taste, the children find solace in the minor, mirrored details. And the music of fatality.

17

In stop-motion animation, the professor floats across the linoleum earth, arms and legs dangling from his rotund frame like heavy chunks of deadwood. He can feel the weight of the sun on his fat, bristled neck. Disposable nightmares flit across his mind's screen as he devolves into a Hyde-like prodigy, withered and ragged and rife with glory, before the wet eyes of the creator, who realizes that a so-called Jekyll never existed in the first place: this current facsimile is the original prototype. Confined to the Yard of the theater with the other proles, Starke laughs at this veritable punchline as he is killed again, resurrected again, killed again, etc., etc., in imaginative and superstylized ways. Patriotism is only as good as the special effects used to reify the arithmetic of its enactment.

18

The outsider slips into a nonrefundable dream where his lines are continually edited out. He can feel the lines tunneling up his esophagus and rolling across his tongue. Then, the moment before articulation, they pixelate in his mouth and evaporate into his nasal cavity. Who is responsible? The outsider searches for the culprit, riding up and down the elevators, running through the streets. He discovers a partisan film crew in room 18 of the Blue Motel shooting what is ostensibly a pornographic movie. Each member of the crew holds an antiquated smartphone over his head like a torch and records a man and a woman having sex on a cum-stained mattress from precarious down-angles. The man's thick, feathered, tennis-pro hair complements the woman's gleaming arugula. The outsider imagines the outcome of a bigot raid, but ultimately aggression of any kind doesn't make sense and won't be productive. He slips aside, revises his agenda, and remembers who he is: Starke, man of the crowd. An integer without an equation.

19

The lounge and the motel have been evacuated by the local authorities, who ferried the slot machines away in wheelbarrows and replaced the deluxe shower mats with unfolded, unread newspapers. Today's headlines all concern the matter of history, viz., how history doesn't matter, how nothing changes, how the universe was never born and will never die. Time always finds a way to reinvent itself. Ghosts always find a way to haunt the stars. Concerned, the fisherman glances back and forth between the headlines and a sign on the wall that reads NO CLEANING FISH IN THE SHOWER. Naturally, he disobeys the sign, like all of the motel guests, but he ignores the lounge, unable to enjoy himself in the absence of gambling devices, even if the lounge and the motel have been evacuated by the local authorities, and nobody, including the fisherman, is there.

20

Weary and disjointed, the director hijacks the pathology of his leading man, then shoots him in the head and commandeers the role. He films himself with a sentient IMAX camera that has not yet been invented and only exists in select futures. During a dream sequence, a league of corpuscles flows into the aqueduct where he falls asleep after a gunfight. The weird individuality of the corpuscles belies their affection for community and togetherness. With no warning, the scene scatters outward like birdshot. Viewers realize that the dream of the rood was a joke written by a medieval stand-up comedian. The rabble burned him at the stake for cheap jokes and bad stage presence. Centuries later, another child dances into the intersection and receives an ovation from the ghosts of tomorrow. Finally the professor returns to the observatory and contemplates the nature of the director's ontology. Gazing into the telescope, he observes what appears to be a coven of nosferatu haranguing Starke on a rogue channel. In fact, they are elderly male actors in frock coats asking Starke for directions to oblivion. If only it were that simple. In a different context, these diegeses might be guilty as charged. Another exertion could render them practical.

Alex Checkovich

'71's

<u>12 | 16 | 40</u>. Then I'm probably praying, *Just give me a cool drink of water before I diiie*, that *be-* in apostrophe-free *before* crucifying a crucial comus since I'm not Maya Angelou, haven't even heard of her, tbh—

—"You gonna order *what*," the dealer barks. Another **first utterance**. To his "helper." Good. Inconspicuous, diligent, I nose back—

—down, **deep in the smothering blackness**, and yay, meh, **Lee May**, borders beginning to teem teeny indeed.

<u>560 | 9 | 15</u>. Everyone here's a white guy, o/c. Paunchers from Brooklyn and Yonkuhz… Mid-lifers named Lenny and **Rusty**, Cohen and **Staub**… I know these guys. I know their bricks: Led Zep and the Stones, Pink Floyd and Jethro Tull, time-locked **songs of love and hate**. Ms. Angelou's no white guy. What else might our Orb stack, **beneath the weight / Of our absent selves**, what alternative acoustic spaces, other orbits that've organized breath?

<u>439 | 39 | 4</u>. Mom's not here, o/c; she never attended shows. She'd blurt, "Ach, those lousy Beatles," before crossly turning the dial. Against Phillies telecasts, she'd spurt, "Ach, lousy **Luzinski**, he's such a sausage," before nosing back into her crosswords. Those carols were king: a **tapestry** I adored. This Luzinski's off-center ("o/c"); we'll pass. "We'll"—as if my father's swooning the same sudden ravenousness? Mmmm, snack-bar sausages, **plump and tender with navy bean sullenness**.

544 | 10 | 13. Some Americans in '71 undoubtedly experienced two freshnesses playing simultaneously: **Vida Blue** and Joni's *Blue*. Only the Orb knows who, how many, how. Lydia Davis re-minds, "We don't see wholes, we see fragments." '71—one orbit—was, for our blue Orb, a mere bit. **Seeing all / I saw the colors fade / And change**. "Therefore, in this case, as in others, it is the reader also making the work, seeing…"

630 | [NR] | 8. Wouldn't a church basement make a random house for a baseball card show? Perhaps. But consider other orbiting arbitraries. **Roberto Clemente** ('34-'72): doomed immortal, so kinetically lithe, juxtaposed against day-glo plastic seats. Benjamin Britten ('13-'76): doomed conductor of Bach's *St. John Passion* – sung in English. **Ritual on my lips / I** [b. '76] **lie in stolid hopelessness / And they lay my soul in strips**. Weren't we all praying for "finds"?

17 | 13 | 503. *Just Give Me a Cool Drink of Water 'fore I Diiie* (Random House, '71) is "the first collection of poems by African-American writer and poet Maya Angelou." Her visage smolders intently from the VG-EX cover. Thumbin' thru tattered pages—poems, cards—each **a door of chance / That leads to a world in question**. Writhing within my funkadelicatessen **maggot brain**, Motown slugger **Gates Brown** seems sad, wise, moonfaced: a male Maya.

3 | 180 | 19. All I want's tago home. Can we? Please, Papa. He doesn't understand. On yr feet, the heat, three+ hours, jostling amongst human stacks, quiddity their fetididdity, why'd I wear this itch-puffin starch-jacket inta church, blurt it **"Tago Mago"** splurt it all single syllable-like like **"Alkaline"** battery acid God lezzjus 180 outta here, yaknow Wawago home, c'mon this table: *clearly* diminishing returns, **sad and wise / Decisions** c'mon, let's move ahhhhn, Father!

<u>99 | 20 | 593</u>. Topps's workaday dilemma: how to imbue 752 black-bordered cardboard rectangles with pleasing proportions of photographic variety (and unity). And you thought Queneau had it tough, telling the same quotidian tale in 99 ways! Stoppin' short—99, shortstop **Mark Belanger**. Is it *really* "near mint"? **Doubt and fear, / Ungainly things**… Oulipo's stark promise: **natural black inventions: root strata**. Or, this bit: through constraints—conservative as Kirk—comes liberation—radical as Rahsaan.

<u>525 | 53 | 7</u>. "I'll never forget," recalls *Forbes*'s David Seideman, "seeing **Ernie Banks** in the mid-1980s at a baseball card show at the Armenian Church on Manhattan's East Side…. He was sitting at a table signing photos and other objects while singing 'Stormy Weather,'" shuffling songbinders of **America**. *Fa-(la)-hey-eyyy*…! So it *wasn't* just my imagination! **You come to me, unbidden / Beckoning me / To long-ago rooms, / Where memories lie** like Ernie's eyes.

<u>26 | 1 | [NR]</u>. Guy Davenport's roster of "communal genius": "French cuisine, Cretan stubbornness, Sotch skepticism…"—Armenian churchitecture?—"…Dutch housekeeping." Fingerin' fragments... Hey! **Rik Aalbert Blijleven**'s rookie card! Curveballer: dike-scraping fingers; **said my house was licking clean**. Delightfully, on *Live in Berlin '71*, Dutch oddball Han Bennink—"the most pro-active percussionist in jazz history"—pitches detritus everywhere. Through what dis/orderly sociocorporeal orb-bits of Career could a *Hollander* have ever made America's majors? Who were "Armenians"?

<u>5 | 150 | 29</u>. "'71's" as in *Contraction*: "seventy-one is" an entity, a prime number, an arbitrary year. "'71's" as in *Possession*: it owns Papa and me right now, rite teeming hear in this church—

—"'71'[?]s!?" woofs the dealer. To another customer. A **gruffish gesture altering** our browsing conditions, sudden as **Sam McDowell**. "Dunno, you'll haveta *check*."

So now, pressure. Not just grammatical. Sociocorporeal. Each card: *Yea-or-Nay*. Can we divine any talismans. Are we **Faust**.

<u>2 | 12 | 15.</u> 1.) 6/12/70: cool-as-hell Pirate **Doc Ellis** pitches a no-hitter—whilst trippin' on LSD. Nonfiction. 2.) x/x/80-something: to get tested for hypoglycemia, I must consume a king-sized Hershey's Symphony bar in five minutes. I manage only 71%. Poetry. 3.) x/x/90-something: Inside that hothouse church basement let's Alice-glass myself. There: my disembody **jabs ceaselessly at phantoms / In the room**, ecstatic **journey in Satchidananda** where sober-as-hell hormones heap hallucinogenic coal trains, debilitating. Truth.

<u>11 | 436 | [NR]</u>. When pinprick mint, '71s absolutely scintillate. Their celebrated/ castigated borders: black as jet; heartbreakingly easy to mar. **Neither touch nor / Care to touch**… One teeny scuff, one stray attic-orbit, and telltale wightwood leers forever. (Witness this dog-eared **Wilbur Wood**.) Talking *fractions* of inches. Like collectors' ancient vinyl record-sleeves: balmy surfaces, buh-uhtttt… o/c… blunted corners. You'll never find the LP, *Ichnos*, that "adventurous vehicle for Oxley's pin-sharp sound," on CD. Dogged pursuits.

<u>6 | 14 | 90</u>. **What's going on?** I'm with my father, underneath NYC's Armenian Church, attending a card show in the early '90s (or late '80s?). Those numbers need apostrophes? Don't ask **the commoners who genuflect and cross their fingers**, pilgrim-consumers herein, blob-arrays, Mikes & Mahvins hobbyin' gay. And perhaps, just as Non Phixion apostrophizes **"Joe Pepitone"** on the P.A., we're scrutinizing an actual Pepitone—Papa

and I, hunched over a binder of half-promising '71s.

<u>18 | 20 | 17</u>. There's three rules. (Grammar, miles **down its trackless wastes**, K's like **Reggie Jackson**.) 1.) Each entry's first sentence must showcase one(+) apostrophe. 2.) Each entry must binder 71 words. ("/"s count…?) 3.) Each entry must be boldly/ graphically appropriate: a '71 LP; a '71 Topps; a prayer-fragment from one of the 20 poems comprising Book One of Angelou's '71 opus. Why *those* arbitraries? Sounds, Images, Language. Fundamental orb-bricks even **Jack Johnson** couldn't K.O.

<u>5 | 145 | 10</u>. Hypoglycemia's symptoms include weakness, irritability, lush swooning harmonics, and an overwhelming desire to hover horizontally like this stereoscopic panorama of doomed captain **Thurman Munson** ('47-'79), the set's most desirable card. If burdened with rescuing *just one* recording from the shipwreck'd dreck of '71, I'd most desire *Voyager*'s extraterrestrial emissary, ***Java: Court Gamelan***. Cavernous atmos congenial to birdsong… stately carillons languidly tolling Time's languid oscillations… **blue farewell / Of a dying dream**.

<u>19 | 9 | 393</u>. Because they're "nature…"—Orb bits—"…transformed," baseball cards are, like nearly *every single thing*, merely technologies. Greasy dealuhzs, Morty Feldmans gazin' outta tables… This thing I'm re-collecting? It ain't exactly an early-'90s monologue. It's a hi-tech 20[-]20 stereologue, replete with *ex post facto* quadrophenia wherein some present-day sentience—"Barry Bonds"—reconstructs his/my own prior incarnation— Papa/**Bobby Bonds**, shuffling **half-truths told and entire lies**, right here, **false relationships and the extended ending**.

<u>380|63|2</u>. '71's orbit. What, truly, constitutes "a year"? Momentsexperiencessnapshots— stacking infinitely up. Labors, bricks, Armenianisms constituting just this *one* building; God, too many bindings. Here's **Ted Williams**—wait. He retired in '60! *Senators* hat?

Oh. "Manager." Hate that. And every time you glimpse other showcases—desultory '88 Toppses thisaway, stacka '54s there, ***dez anos depois***— you're collapsing entire *years*. **My shroud of black be weaving** flushing crushing Nara Leão blushing slushing—sick.

<u>600 | 6 | 28</u>. "'71's" as in *Folk Grammar*, as in *Found Material*. It's the dealer's hand-Sharpied label for what's in this binder. I'd never make *his* mistake! I ain't worldly like Gil-Scott, name-dropping **Willie Mays** on his revolutionary anthem—God no; *other*worldly sugar-slush hormones're *here*—but I do know *that*. Why? Cuz it's my single core credential… **my evening's joy**… my 710 on the S.A.T. (verbal). **That's pieces of a man** hypoglycemia k'neau K.O.!

<u>70 | 154 | 3</u>. This entire endeavor's failed.

—dealer (hairy, parched, dogged): "Entire *what*—"

—SHADDUP.

(Delusion of the fury.)

This binder-plunder: utterly fruitless. **Cesar Gutierrez**'s dream to K.O. *just one* MLB homer. This church's resolve to overawe. This yearning to transmute my suffering to Papa. These recordings—prose-poems—dog-eared black-edged snapshots—of "events." **This clean mirror / Traps me unwilling / In a gone time—**

—Any arbitrary numbered year, *in itself*, cannot fail. True?

Ngozi Oparah

Swallow

Swallow

1. cause or allow (something, especially food or drink) to pass down the throat.
2. believe unquestioningly (a lie or unlikely assertion).
3. perform the muscular movement of the esophagus required to do this, especially through fear or nervousness.
4. put up with or meekly accept (something insulting or unwelcome).
5. resist expressing (a feeling) or uttering (words).
6. take in and cause to disappear; engulf.
7. completely use up (money or resources).

"Swallow" definitions from Oxford, via Google.

1.

I like this. The waiting we have us doing. The almost, near, that we keep living in. A pause as time moves, brushing against us. I like the way it feels to want something that I've never met, never had, never tasted. I like the recklessness it creates in me. I would damage anything to have it, taste it, you.

We meet online and I only like one of your pictures. The one where your hands cover half your face. Your hair is the brown that I call blonde and your eyes are blue. You are white. And I have been chasing a difference that destroys my whole life. So you are perfect.

I think you feel the same. I think you love the in-between as much as I do. I want to say that this might be better than the getting. But that would be a lie for the sake of poetry. If I believed that, that the almost was as good as the it, then this almost wouldn't be what it is. And it is.

I am an easy target. I make myself this way.

I practice the way your tongue tastes on mine every night we don't reunite. If I close my eyes, I can count the bumps that give you flavor. And your hands, I have made them my own for now. Choreographed copies: Touch neck, Touch chin, inside me.

You rub me as if there is something underneath. Something to unearth. Anything more. As if this skin was the dust atop what you were after. You will ruin me trying to find me.

I haven't been able to replicate your voice. The way man can't create earthquakes. The way I can't give my own body chills. You are silent in memories. The silence suffices. Your smile, however, is imprinted. All of its versions. The halves and quarters and fourths. The one independent of me, the one induced with kisses on lips or chest or neck or thigh.

They are all here with me now. Splayed out like first apartment posters, a housewarming.

You couldn't find the cafe I suggested. You text me 15 minutes before I'm supposed to see you for the first time asking, wondering if it is all a trap. I worry the same as I open your text.

It doesn't exist, you say, with just enough context to have it apply to me and you in several ways. It does, I promise. I just saw it, just walked by it, almost entered the other day. They call it something different now, but all the insides are the same.

You are there before me. I know it as I approach. Every step closer to you might be the first you see of me. I am aware of this. I walk with my shoulders forced back and hold my lips tight against my face. I pretend I am complete. I wish I would have had a drink before I see you. I worry you'll see the parts of me that can only be loved with time.

I ask my mind to ignore the pieces of living that have nothing to do with you. Recruit all energy to cause your resurrection. I shut myself down in this way. Make a spotlight for my consciousness.

We are down the street from where we started. Two pints deep into knowing each other. I am loose enough to touch you now. Leg against yours, hand against bare skin. Laughs bring my cheek to your chest. Eye contact until it asks to be something else. I look to see who's watching. Hoping this memory won't be just mine. That we are large enough to make a history outside ourselves.

I won't take you home tonight. I mantra silently while kissing every public inch of you. I am performing the part of good. Even though it hurts. Even though it's not for folks like us, not for times like now.

I wonder why strangers can know this body better. You touch it like you knew exactly how it was to be used. More aware of its needs. The ease of your entry confuses me.

> *I want to shove your hand down my throat. Consume you. Your salty finger suffices. Even though we have moved to the furthest corner of the dark dive bar, we can still be seen. The older white woman across the way, across the table sees me chewing on your nail beds and shakes her head in jealousy. I pity those forced to watch this sort of magic from afar.*

I don't want this to be a poem. Nor diary. I don't mean to talk about you like confession, like secret, or like song. I want to be able to speak of you in common language so I don't burn for idolization. I wish this to be a list. Sheepishly, sloppily drawn on reused paper. No importance by looks. The language you require makes this near impossible. How do you speak of gold without naming it? What's missing when you do? It. Is. You are not gold, I don't mean to confuse myself. In fact, you are more important. Gold and I have never met, never touched. I have not longed for gold for the past 13 nights. I have not stayed wide awake pleading gold's name while inside myself, while in sleep. You are not gold.

> *I want for every sentence you utter to include me. I want signs I have corrupted your future in the ways you've sullied mine. Your shoulder brushes against me and you threaten to hold my hand. We are still sitting and I worry I won't know what to do with it once I have to carry it.*

> *You trace the lines on the backside of each knuckle. You tell me I'm long and thin. I take this as a compliment because I've learned thin means beautiful to folks who look*

like you.

You press the bottom of your palm against mine and I panic. Soon you'll see that my hands are longer, bigger than yours. This will make you feel small in a way men are not supposed to.

I curl my fingers inwards so that your hands can fold over mine. Disappear me. You will not learn yet that you are not as large as me. I will keep it a secret for as long as we can.

2.

It's before date three and outsiders are starting to worry where I've been and since when I require your permission, your presence to exist. Everything I own smells like you. I make a new habit of ducking my nose into the inside of my shirt collar. I do this, too, when you are around. Double up on you. Retreat into the you of you that's mine.

The last time we meet, you meet my friends. I go with them to the first bar that welcomed me when I moved to this city. I don't have to show I.D. or pay anymore. I'm there without you because you are busy when we leave. I burrow my face in my dress and text you of each move I make. When you arrive, you exchange hellos and take me from their night. I am elated to be seen with you. To be whisked away to better things. I walk slowly and loudly as we leave. To cause a ruckus of us. Make sure everyone has a chance to stare and wonder where it is we were going, coming from. As their eyes meet ours, I wonder if they think you are more beautiful than me. It wouldn't surprise me if they did, all of them. You have the looks we are taught to want. Your hair moves with the wind and your eyes catch light to reveal what eyes are made of. Everyone would want to be you. Being with you is the best form of losing.

I mouth, he's mine when eyes find their way to me. I furrow my brows which makes me uglier. More dangerous. You put your fingers between mine and pull me out, away. I feel leashed. I close my eyes and practice trust without your permission. You pass a test you never knew you were taking.

I'm wet for you by the time we reach the car.
Your friends are cool, you tell me.
And I laugh.
This confuses you.
So I stop. Straighten my face. Regret. You believe that you know them enough from the two minutes you spoke to them.
You think so? I ask, erasing.
Yeah. They're cool.

I take your right hand and put it to my throat.
You welcome the distraction. We treat it like the apology I owe you.

I want to tell you that I haven't been able to stop thinking about you. That these thoughts range from masturbation, mostly masturbation, to some idealized future where I'm asking you something more intense than I feel comfortable thinking or saying or writing and recording. I looked it up on Google. This means I'm desperate. But I don't feel desperate. Or rushed or in any sort of hurry. I think I want a new word to capture this feeling. *Excitement* is the closest I can get. It's less and more than that. It's less about you exciting me: B acting on A and more A acting on A in B's presence. The word also isn't *inspiration*. I just like who I am when I like you.

The windows fog up from us. I'm breathing too much, too loudly. The steam isn't equal parts yours and mine. I hold my breath as you enter me with two fingers so that everything we create is fair.

I like the space this crush creates to look at myself. I like that I'm getting all dressed up to go get coffee. In case I see you. In case there are more yous roaming around this earth. I like that I've run every day. And enjoy it. Long for it. Maybe the word involves hope. B engenders hope in A, makes it easier for A to touch it, rub against it, pick it up and know that it's true, worth having and keeping around.

When you exit, I am all over you. You say, don't waste it, so close that my ear's hanging edge moves with every syllable.
What should I do? I beg the question.
You look at me and I stop. Again. So the air is all yours, trade for the chance to feel seen like this.

You slide your fingers down so my lip drags against my chin.
I am salt. I am stone.
How do you taste, you whisper, still staring.

And I can't answer cause I can't breathe.

I want to tell you this. But the deeper I think into it, the more clearly it presents itself as not about you. I try and siphon all the power out of you and call you a lesson. Call you a tool of God. The universe's way of putting me back in alignment with the things I want for myself. Balance beam walk to pleasure. I like who I am right now. Even the annoying, obsessive, ask everybody if I should say this insecure parts. I like them.

I gag on your fingers. Drool from both sides of my mouth falls on my chest. Your forearm.
We are leaking.

I feel so adored and more importantly, I feel worthy of total adoration.

You grab the side of my face with wet palms. I smile because I know what comes next.

With you, I can see my beauty and how interesting and funny I am. Feel it rather than know it. Now, I am an accessible truth.

You help me feel every bone of my throat. The flesh between. I learn of tendons again. Jaw. Neck. Collar. Fight.
You hold me until my eyes shut, still open, without me.
You forget, because the windows are fogged and we cannot see the streets, because the heat of us is audible and we cannot hear the smoking crowd inches from our haven, that we are still in public.

3.

For our third date, I ask you to meet me in my room. In my bed. I will either wear a one-piece lingerie suit I bought for my ex or my running shorts and a crop top with no bra.

When you cancel last minute, I am already covered in makeup and anticipation. I chose the shorts and feel foolish. As if somehow, the universe made you cancel for my poor decision making.

I question everything.

Can't tonight, sorry. Is all you think to text me.
I question. Every thing.
I mantra that I've already seen you for the last time and soak myself in mourning. I
ruin my sheets.

I had a vivid dream with all the same players from the night. So I can't tell what was real, what was imagined anymore. Soft reflections of each other and I don't know where to land, where I landed. If I landed. The part where he loved me. The part where he said, I love you, to both eyes at once. That was a dream. The part where I begged him to enter again and again as hard as he could. That was real. Much realer than I imagined I could be with such a near-stranger.

4.

My best friend has alerted me that my infatuation is a result of my desperation, the generalized longing that has lived with me ever since I was a self. If I agree with her aloud, I am afraid my body will fall into this version of me, this truth, and never recover. So I reject each of her words from now on.

On my way, you say a week later, send me your address.
It is night and I have not heard from you for more than 100 characters since you
dropped me off after choking me. After you stood me up. Left me waiting. Waning.

I plan to respond with, "We should talk about what happened."
I think that I could guilt you into staying around longer than you should.
I know, though, guilt doesn't work on men like you unless it comes from within.
So I cancel my plans and disappointment and I send you my address.

I've been feeling windful—a version of empty with edges, balloon body. Best friend and I speak of how sex feels only as long as it is happening. Upon exit, I am again a bag. Barren. As I cum, I feel my return. I feel all the ways I still want the one inside me to be inside/against/me/my puppeteer. I want to beg to be held, to feel the heat of these men for longer than their bodies can remain warm. I want something I cannot name and they cannot provide.

You are horny by the time you arrive.
You can't help it. I'm so damn sexy, you say.
Your dick is hard as proof, you show me. Make me touch it.
I smile, but we are moving too fast for me to be there.

They always leave. Me. I'm not sure I want them to stay. Some version of them, yes, the feeling they bring, yes. But their composite beings are not enough. Even as they ram all that they have to offer in me over and over again. Even as I beg for harder faster thicker longer versions of this punishment, watch the sweat collect on the sides of their naked bodies, above quick-exhaling mouths, even as I open and clench and stretch all of me in willful receipt, I am wanting. I am always wanting.

I don't want you to think, you say.
Against the coldest wall of my darkened room, you place my cheek and whisper for me to leave you alone with me.

And this is your version of foreplay
To make a doll of me
Statue.
Zombie.
Less.on.

5.

I don't or can't remember what happened the last time he was here. I know a few things for sure. But they are less memories than the childhood stories parents tell about a self before it starts to be. Our sex was unprotected. His dick struggled to do what dicks do, or should, and remain hard. We opened at least one condom, used none. Someone, likely myself, attempted to throw a condom wrapper in the trash beside my desk and failed (this fact was assumed the morning after).

> *I wake up beside you and I am vibrating. I am swollen. Swelling. I know that I have been loved. Am being.*

The sex, despite all tragedies—forgotten and remembered—was quite remarkable. I smiled through most of it. My cheek hurt the following morning as confirmation. He made me feel. The way he touched me brought to life something. Fully.

These are likely lies.

They felt too easy to write. What is true is that I drank an entire bottle of corner store Sauvignon Blanc in preparation for our meeting. When the bottle finished and my words and vision began to slur, I still felt insufficient. I rifled through my friend's and sister's things and made myself a cocktail consisting of moonshine and some other white wine. I replaced my borrowings with warm tap water and pray no one will ever find out. I realize I can be a thief, my desperation makes this so. I waited drunkenly for him, half naked and expecting to be out of my mind by the time we met.

> *I ask you to rip the lingerie off of me, but it is too strong. You are too weak to ruin the memories of the men that precede you.*
> *I can never be naked again.*

I do want to remember. Not so I can sit in the imagery, but so that I can tell myself that I was there. That I was in control during those hours. I want record of being animate.

Being more than body, I'm not sure why I so easily give myself up to these men. Why I curate me in half for lovers who never know me better than a stranger. How do I keep convincing myself that this is what I want, even if just for a moment?

> *I draft a text to you after you leave. It stays in the box below your name for days. Neither of us interrupt my process.*
> *I erase my "what happened" texts, trade it for "what's up?"*
>
> *I am not ready to lose*
>
> *We go on one more date before I flee.*

I remember meeting him at the brewery. And having him put his hand on my lap as he talked to his friend about business.

> *I am the purse you put on the chair. Check I'm there in panicked, drunken intervals. Save a seat for no one.*

I remember feeling impressed, excited that he knew so much about something I knew nothing of.

> *Three times, quick, five fingers on left thigh. You pat me down, back in place when I move to pee.*

I was the only woman in our company. I was the only black person in our group. I wonder if his friends thought me his plaything.

> *When I introduce myself. Extend my hand to be touched. I see them forgetting me. I fumble my name on purpose, so I am unintelligible, so you have to ask to hear it again if I'm to be kept. They nod, smiles concave, grateful their time with me is over. You let this happen. You help this happen.*

I wasn't offended that they might. I relished the label, being assumed an object. Purely. For aesthetics.

> *When you chose me as your object, you proved to me I was worth owning*
> *At the time, this was more than enough for me.*

> *Your friends leave and I invite you over, intent on remembering.*

6.
Our sex is unprotected.

> *I want to be scarred by you.*

Be   cause
I, especially when intoxicated, cannot access, cannot trust in my own permanence.

> *I whisper, do whatever you want, when you're on top of me. In the wet salt of your ears. Your eyes are closed so you can see the me you want most.*

> *You nod with furrowed brows and hilled skin, cause freedom, this permission, has*

never been part of the fantasy for you.
You roll over and you are
we are
finished.

And I am
Still.

7.

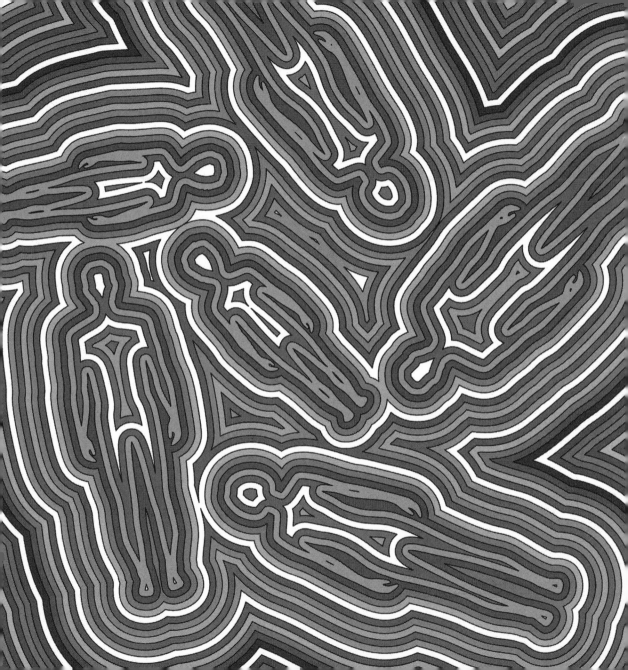

KKUURRTT

Advanced Praise for *Fiction International 53*: Algorithm (as auto-generated by Botnik Predictive Writer)

"Wow, I have learned admirably of our headlong views through another time."
— Elizabeth Stockton, *Tone Creation*

"Would recommend this for sustainable imagery today with our regular writing market."
— Naomi Sentence, *One Word Annual*

"Every incredible detail is an electric debut by author."
— Whitney Morgenstern, *Romance Devices*

"Throughout social memory lies required literary spectacle of which hopefully this is."
— Emily Knopf, *Culture Change*

"This is beautifully written thematic publishing of all things between each adjoining important."
— David 'Feature' Anker, *The Georgiana Kid*

"Across the globe until which hopefully there is no longer anything quite so compelling to read."
— Malcolm W. President, *The Book That Should*

"That is smart."

— You

"Book reader praise for understanding why extremely talented."
— BJ Northington, *Artificially Induced Synthesis*

Kenneth Calhoun

The White Woman

The name assigned to William's particular LearningLady was Camila. The marketing team had selected it from a list of most popular female names in Mexico. William was to refer to his unit by name and to use female pronouns. This not only served the illusion of her personhood—since *she* would no longer be referred to as an *it*—but also helped direct the deep learning algorithms seeking gender-specific content to supplement the behavioral datasets.

Camila sat next to him in the hired car as they made their way out of the sprawling Federal District and were soon lifted by the winding road into the neighboring range. For the moment, the driver, Manuel, had given up trying to identify her. He had recognized her face, but couldn't pin down where he had seen her before. He insisted that he knew her from somewhere.

William had wondered if this would be the case among the locals. It was, after all, by design. When they first received the invitation from the Mexican government to demo the LearningLady, the robotics team had a brainstorming session with cultural customization in mind. What adjustments could they make to their female-chassis teaching robots that would have irresistible appeal on the other side of the Wall, where teachers were needed in rural communities? They wanted to do a focus group, but Spanish-speaking people did not respond to the call for fear of being deported. It was hard, during those early months of the round-ups, to find people from anywhere in Central America, let alone Mexico. CTO Dan eventually brought in a very tired looking man—someone he claimed he had picked up outside a Home Depot. Many doubted this since the practice had more or less been eliminated by the sweeps. Rather, they assumed that the man was secretly employed and housed by Dan at his sprawling avocado farm in Fallbrook.

The man's name was Rey. He was in his early-50's, had grown up in Ciudad Juarez, and claimed to have traveled to America around 2002, though his English was still curiously limited. They brought Rey to the East Lab and showed him the Lady prototypes, which he looked upon with horror, crossing himself as he took in their exposed mechanics, the spaghetti of wiring spilling out of unsealed binding.

"Who," they asked him, "is the most admired woman in Mexico?"

He reportedly answered that the most admired woman in all of Mexico was Madonna, William later learned. This satisfied the technicians initially, but later, after they had released Rey, realized they weren't sure which Madonna he meant. Was it the Lucky Star Madonna of the early-80's, the Material Girl, True Blue Madonna, Vogue Era Madonna or even the more recent Rebel Heart Madonna that appeared at the Super Bowl, flanked by Nikki Minaj and M.I.A.? Unsure they dressed up the LearningLadies in each of the star's personas and asked the CTO to bring back Rey, despite their concerns that some of the Madonnas were inappropriate for the classroom. We can't apply our own standards for decency to their culture, they reminded themselves.

Rey was shown the Madonnas like a victim surveying a police line-up. He shook his head violently.

"No?" the engineers asked.

"No, no," he said. "Absolutamente no!" He said other things they could not catch. Only one word was picked up by Sales Director Jerry, the Grenada Invasion vet who had heard, possibly used, the word before: virgen.

"He's saying *virgin*," Jerry informed the engineers. "You got it all wrong, nerds."

Rey was again released as they went back to the drawing board, this time putting all their energies into outfitting a Lady with the lacy wedding dress and sheer bustier of the Like a Virgin Madonna. Rey was, once again, summoned to the East Lab. When he saw the Lady propped on a worktable, draped with beaded necklaces like Mardi Gras flasher, arms sheathed in long sheer gloves, he grew angry. The foreign words came at the engineers in a lengthy barrage. It was then, as they huddled against Rey's apparently shaming diatribe, that Jerry remembered the guy who drove him to all the karaoke bars in San Diego one night, so he could perform "Baby Got Back" to a variety of audiences. That guy who spoke Spanish. That guy who had told him, as they ate midnight tacos at the Robertos in Carmel Valley, about how he had once translated for some first responders at a crash site he came upon.

"What guy?" the technicians asked.

"A guy. Some guy. Half-something, Asian maybe. Works here. Writes trivia. Bill? Will?"

William was located in the writing bays and brought in. He was sat in front of Rey and, after only a few minutes, understood.

"He doesn't mean Madonna the singer," William clarified. "He means Madonna the saint."

The engineers were confused.

"You know, Mary?" William tried.

Still nothing.

"The Virgin Mary?"

"Wait," Jerry said. "Holy crap. Ha ha ha! Jesus' mom, guys. He means Jesus' mom!"

As they drove on, Manuel pointed out Mt. Popo, the famous volcanic peak that had witnessed the gradual influx of prehistoric humans to the region, the rise of the empire on the lake, the arrival of mounted and armored Europeans and the slaughter that followed them like a wake of blood, then the disappearance of the lake under the city and the disappearance of the city under the smog. The peak, with its snow-streaked sides and broad cone, wore a rakish plume of roiling smoke, a mushroom cloud accessory. It had been active lately, threatening vengeful annihilation at last, in fulfillment of the prophecies. William did not fear an eruption now. His biography had already accommodated the end of democracy in America and, he believed, there was no more room for such significant historical footnotes at the bottom of pages crowded with unexceptional episodes.

He watched Camila, in her periwinkle hoodie scan the landscape, knowing that the apertures of her eyes were taking in the stony formations and that shape-recognition technology was matching contours and ridgelines with the endlessly annotated, crowd-sourced map in her brain-banks. Soon, he noted, they would lose the invisible network tether with the Cloud as they left the city's wired environs, and she would be operating locally. He wondered if he would notice the impairment as he studied her narrow fingers, the delicately sculpted hand resting on her lap—the detail of faint knuckle creases, the subtle array of veins.

The fingers fluttered slightly, as if she was lightly playing a chord on an invisible keyboard. The tiny gesture suggested something like impatience or maybe physiological response to a song stuck in her head—a subtle artistic flourish on part of the designers at Sapient Systems, offering a degree of verisimilitude that never failed to startle William.

"Mira," Manuel said from the front seat. Then in English: "The white woman."

William followed the driver's pointing finger and scanned the roadside. No woman of any color was visible.

"Where's this?" he asked. "Donde?"

"Alla."

This time Manuel kept his hands on the wheel, pointed vaguely with a nod that seemed to accommodate a million miles of exterior. "She sleeps, see?"

William leaned forward and scanned the landscape, both the sparse forest sliding by and the far off, more fixed features of the terrain. "There's a woman?"

"The white woman! There!"

"I don't see a woman, Manuel. Should we stop?"

"Ha ha. No, señor. You cannot wake her."

William found the situation distressing. He continued to scan the shoulder and the woods beyond, leaning forward, the money belts cutting into his ribcage and stomach. What the hell was Manuel talking about?

As if she heard this thought, Camila raised her hand and pointed over the driver's shoulder. "He's referring to Iztaccíhuatl, that volcano there," she said calmly. "Locals see a sleeping woman in the profile of the peaks. See? There is the head, then her hands resting on her chest, her hip and then the rise of her knees. The snow makes her white."

William sighted the collection of suggestive ridges down Camila's arm and beyond the tip of her finger. Yes, he could see the vague shape of a woman's figure in full-body profile.

"The name Iztaccíhuatl means White Woman in Nahuatl and it is the third highest peak in Mexico."

"Si, si," Manuel said, nodding in agreement. "The White Woman."

"The legend goes that she was a princess in love with the great warrior Popocatepetl and that she was promised to him upon his return from battle. But when she heard news that he had been killed in battle, she died of grief. The news was false, however, and when the warrior returned he took her body to this spot and kneeled at her side. Now he was the one to grieve. The gods turned them into mountains and covered them with a blanket of snow. Popocatepetl rages to this day over her death, fuming, threatening to erupt. You see?" She pointed to the column of smoke rising from Mt. Popo.

"Si. She knows," Manuel said, smiling into the mirror. "La profesora."

Camila returned the smile then sat back in her seat, her head turned away so that William could only see the back of her hood. She had delivered this historical narrative in a gentle, teacherly tone, with inflection suited for a classroom of kids.

"Will she ever wake up?" William asked.

Camila turned to him, "It is only a myth, William."

William smiled. "Yes, I know."

She crooked her head and studied him, blinking twice. He felt something being recorded, bookmarked and applied to a dataset. He was watching her learn, but what exactly?

They settled back into their seats and Manuel drove on. The mountains, the White

Woman and her warrior lover, were receding from view. Poor Popo, he thought. Fucked over by Fake News. Fuming like the rest of us.

"Should we stop and get a picture?" William asked no one in particular.

"No stopping here," Manuel said. "There are many bandidos. You understand? Ladrones."

"Ah," William said, scanning the road ahead. "Right. Don't stop."

"I have sent you a picture," Camila said quietly. "To your phone."

William pulled his phone from his pocket and saw that he was still getting a signal, however feeble. He checked his email. Yes, she had used her company account to send him a few attachments, as well as a link to Google images responding to her search query for "views of Mount Popocatepetl." He clicked on the attachment icon and saw the sequence of pictures she had taken from her seat behind Manuel. Over-the-shoulder shots of the mountain, his oddly hairy ear lobe in the frame, captured with the camera in her eyes.

"Thanks, Camila." Using the name like he would Siri or Alexa.

"You're welcome, William." She looked at him and her mouth performed a half-smile, the left corner rising slightly. He mirrored her expression, then they both settled back into their seats.

"I know I know you from somewhere!" Manuel insisted, studying her in the rearview. "You are so familiar to me, profa. It's making me crazy."

Camila responded with a slight tilt of the head.

"Could it be that I saw you once in a dream?" the driver said, turning in his seat.

More like a vision, William thought.

Later they passed a roadside shrine. He caught the face of Our Lady of Guadalupe, peering out of the small shelter, her shoulders draped with a string of dried roses. The driver's head swiveled as they slid past. Maybe now Manuel would make the connection, but he drove on in silence.

AUTOBIOGRAPHER WANTED TO TELL STORY OF MY LIFE IN MY OWN WORDS (CONCISE, TENDER) THAT KEEP
ELUDING ME, REASONABLE FEE PAID FOR THIS UNREASONABLE SERVICE and day after the ad runs th
ere's a line at my apartment door (stretching down the hall) of men and women who have not
worked in years (except in their own minds) (except to record little facts and feelings and
and ideas pertaining to their own lives on little pieces of papers and on the back of post
cards and on napkins too of hourse) and instead of resumes they bring writing samples stuf
stuffed in envelopes and in one case a sock, and Im Amuel, interview them one by one--Keitg
and Marco and Anette and 2893 (she calls herself) and Peter and all the rest (the line has
a reach down the stairs and out the lobby door onto the street and down the street past th
the house Dr. Suess migh t have designed and over the river and through the hall--who know
where the line end--I try not to think about that--I try to respect (handle with respect t
the writing samples scattered in front of me like mindguts and try ta im press on each of
the pototential autobiographers of me the urgency of this drearical writing task (stirn, of
stormthundertormthrorms)--that is, I, Amuel (everyman minus every munis man) tell applican
applifants (can'ts too) that I figure it is time for me to learn something about meself th
that I don't want to know and which can only be revealed by someone who is me and not me--
some collation of wordlings which could cast on my posterity a more positive light, (or a
half-lught, atl ast)--anyway, rinse in the name of TRUTH from my life story the lured-lit
tedness shining now and how, and how. I am blind with seeing, I tell them. You can be--if
you are hired--my laser surgery. "wh at is your previous experience with Timelines!" I ask
and no matter what they answer, how impressively they lie, I assign or plead with tthem to
in the next 24 hours create a sample autobiographical timeline (10 pages max) and come ba
back because I cannot at this early stage of the interveiling process discount the abilitie
abilities of anyone. And they say, nearly every one (over the course of 40 Biblical days)
they say: "You mean I have made it through the first round of interviews and am--am--am--
being CALLED BACK FOR A SECOND INTERVIEW?" and I say yes, that's it, you made it through--
and they are so thankful, and I am so thankful also, because I've never hired anyone in all
my life and need more practice at saying the right thing--for instance/instaunce/instunce
I fail in every case to accurately explain my difficulty with POSTERITYm how we have alays
been strange bedfellows, lived at much farther than an arm's reach, distrust our manna, as
I don't trust the past and it's posterior manueverings to say anything of value about me--
and that suspicioun holds even when (Or especially when) I am Amuel myself speaking of old
days--they need to know that EXPLICTLTY but though I come near to making the point of just
why I need them tobe me for theduration of a ten volume autobiography I don(t quite make t
the point--I Amuel, frankly, am a bit unprofessional or too glad just to have someone to tal
tale-talk to--tell about how as a child in bed at night I envisioned my own ∪BIRTH BIRTH.
dawn and felt the stone coldness of the reality close around my fleshy pillow and then got
worried less about BIRTH than about what my FIRST WORDS woids/words would be to the MIDWIFE
or ConEd gasman--I had so many ideas forFIRST words, all too grand. or too dumb, or hazy in
a way a person should not be--especially a child--the secondaftery they life, Oh yes, I had
reams of FIRST ords that were stiff as jellified fog--for instance: "What do you do when you
are unabandoned? Try to become abandoned. What do you do when you are abandoned? You try to
become unabandoned." Dear gord, a mish mash of--MAN WORDS I kept trying to sort out,which
was like sorting particles of gruel into millions of vibrant categories. My potential atob
autobiographers--in the second interview--when they retu rned their widely fruity timelines
--heard all about my forty plus years of authoring and re-authoryng FIRSTORDS--a task on
glowing int he act of couse left no time to write my autobiography of a FIRSTORD MONGERER--oh
I was a better interviewer during the decond round, but still not sure as to who to hire--
so unsure that I invited ALL APPLICAN'S back for a third interview, which they wre a little
less thrilled about--especially when I requested that they return with another timeline--
this time telling about the lives/life of somehone dear to them--but they all did come back
with their envelopes and hairdos and their shoes and their ambitions to be my autobiographer
and then I praised them all, and hired them all, an army of autobiographers to attack and
defeat (hopefully) the confusion of my life of mad affairs with fears that kept reproducing
more fears and more FIRSTwords and moMidwife-mann chambers and more FIRST meals and more and
more and more crosses that were shishkabobs--heads impaled on all the points atop the roof
of the church where the headless people untered, hand-painted lids over their neck holes--
death clinches on my influences knowing no net was stretched below men--no mother no fathere

--- rock baby cannonelli beans --- spasms of lire --- Guienea --- Eritrea --orzo, ouzo, ohno ---

W
I
S
H

UUU
P
O
N

A

S
N
O
R
T
I
N
G

S
T
A
R
:
:
T
I
M
E
L
I
N
E
S

O
F

O
U
R

L
I
V
E
S

Stephen-Paul Martin

The Phantom Zone

We went online to get the weather. But by mistake, we clicked on our YouTube account, and got footage of children in detention centers on the Rio Grande. They'd been separated from their parents, stuck in unsanitary conditions, forced to sleep in standing-room-only cells on filthy concrete floors, lights on 24 hours a day, no access to showers, soap, toothpaste, or bathroom facilities, plagued by outbreaks of flu, lice, scabies, chicken pox. We saw hundreds of desperate faces pressed against rusty chain-link fences, banging on bars of cells, or pressing handwritten notes against dirty windows begging for help. We'd been hating the President since he first took office in 2016, when he quickly became the most dangerous man in the world, launching one destructive policy after another. But the cruelty of this latest border procedure was beyond everything. We knew something had to be done. We had to get rid of him.

We knew we didn't have the guts to do it ourselves. We felt we had too much to lose, that our lives were worth living. We didn't want Guantanamo or the electric chair. So we came up with a compromise plan, a way to interfere without facing excessive punishment. Of course it would be insufficient. It would leave the President in charge of the world's most destructive nation. But it was better than nothing.

Now we're at his latest political rally, ready for action. I'm going to stand up in the middle of the President's speech and shout insults at him, targeting his worst abuses of power. Amy will be off to the side, filming it with her phone. She'll post it on YouTube, where it's certain to go viral. I planned on getting an aisle seat, so that after I finished my verbal assault, I could duck out and hide in the bathroom, slip out through the window undetected. But we got there late and the only seat I could find was right in the middle, ten rows back from the stage. So now I'm stuck, no easy way out, surrounded by people eager to support the worst president in U.S. history.

The guy on my right has a shirt with a coiled snake that says Don't Tread on Me. I can tell by his backwards baseball hat and the expression on his face that he owns guns and a pit bull, drives an F-250, never lets people finish their sentences, and thinks that watching Fox News makes him an expert on everything. I know he'll be cheering whenever the President talks about how great his term in office has been. In fact, he's probably been to other Presidential rallies and already knows what the President is going to say. The President won't really say anything, but people like this guy won't care. In fact, they won't even know that the President is just making noise. It won't occur to them that he's supposed to do anything else. It won't occur to the President that he's supposed to do anything else. After all, he got elected making noise a few years ago. Why would he change what worked?

The room itself, normally a high school auditorium, is filled with folding plastic chairs in front of a stage made of risers. Eight big screen TV monitors have been installed, and college football games fill the room. I assume that once the President begins, the games will disappear and the TVs will start broadcasting his speech, as if we can't fully take in what he's saying without simultaneous picture tube versions of it. Or maybe the games will remain, as if to say that the United States is like a football team, competing to be number one.

The lights flick off and on. The football games disappear, replaced by a shot of the podium and American flags on both sides of it. I'm not sure why they need two flags. I'm not sure why they need even one.

I must have a disturbed look on my face because the woman on my left nudges me and asks me why I bothered to show up if I hate the President so much.

Hate? I say.

It's obvious, she smiles. Her form-fitting white uniform makes her look like she might be a nurse in a pornographic movie. She's got a sky-blue name tag that says Randi.

I say: Don't you hate him too?

Not as much as you do.

Why not?

I've been trying to give him a chance. I've been working to convince myself that he's trying to do a job he's not really suited for.

I smile and say: You must be the nicest person in the world. I think he's just an ego-tripping monster.

I agree that he's a jerk, but could you do any better if you were the President?

I'd never be foolish and arrogant enough to run for public office. Anyone who wants to be elected shouldn't be. In fact, they should be regarded as dangerous people.

That's kind of extreme, isn't it?

No more extreme than our current situation.

So why are you even here?

I'm not sure what to say. If I tell her the truth, she might report me, and I might end up in an interrogation room, where tough guys with mirror shades would beat me up, trying to get me to confess that I'm working with a secret organization, even though I'm not. It's true that this will probably happen anyway, after I stand up and shout insults at the President, but I don't want to be apprehended in advance, before I've had the chance to exercise my provisional freedom of speech. She's waiting for me to say something, and from the look on her face I can tell that she's not sure why I'm not responding to her simple question, so I say the only thing I can think of.

Would you blow me later?

What? Did I hear that right?

Probably.

That's really offensive.

Is it? Why is it offensive? You can just say no. Or yes, if you're up for it.

I don't know you at all. In fact, I'm pretty sure now that I don't want to know you.

Why do you need to know me to give me a blow job?

The guy beside me gives us a dirty look and tells us to shut up, nodding toward the microphone fifty feet in front of us, where a fat guy in a tropical shirt is tapping the microphone, trying to get people to stop making noise so the President can start making noise. For a few seconds, I study Randi's face. I feel stupid for having offended her, especially with Amy less than fifty feet away. Sometimes things just pop out of my mouth, and I can't make them disappear, so I act like I meant to say them. Then I think of her compassionate view of the President. It's certainly true that if I became President, I would do a terrible job, and in that sense he and I have something in common. I try to think of other similarities, things he and I both like, but only two things come up: Oreos and pornography. I've heard that whenever he stays in a hotel he insists on having huge amounts of junk food waiting in his room, including 48 family size packs of Oreos, arranged on his bed in six rows of eight (not eight rows of six). I've also heard that he doesn't like being the President because they won't let him watch his porn in the Oval Office. There's something almost charming about the stupidity of the man's obsessions. But in all other ways he just seems mean, self-absorbed, offensive, sociopathic, the kind of guy you might meet in a bar, who would stand too close to you and talk loudly in your face, not letting you finish a single sentence, repeatedly jabbing your chest with a meaty index finger. It's true that if I were bumbling my way through a job I couldn't really do, I'd probably want lots of Oreos and pornography. But I know that unlike the President my way of botching things would be more self-destructive than destructive, like the stupid thing I just said about getting a blow job. I can see a faint smile on Randi's face, as if she's secretly amused by the thought of putting a stranger's dick in her mouth.

She says: Normally, I'd probably think that you're just another stupid fuck. But the guy we'll be listening to a few minutes from now will make you sound like a genius.

I thought you were trying to be compassionate.

I always start that way. But then the guy starts talking, and I totally hate him. I came prepared this time. I'm going to make him lose track of what he's saying.

He'll do that anyway.

Yeah, but it'll be more fun if I *make* him do it. I like making arrogant guys lose their cool.

This guy never had any cool to lose.

The lights flash off and on again. The guy beside me tells me to shut the fuck up. I want to tell him to shut the fuck up. But there's no point in starting a fight with a guy who looks like he likes to start fights.

I review what I'm planning to say. I'm going to let the President get about five minutes into his speech, then stand up and fire off a series of carefully prepared condemnations, speaking loudly but calmly, trying to seem as intelligent and rational as possible, refusing to let him interrupt and talk over me, saying as much as I can before anyone can react and shut me up. I'll tell him he's a complete asshole for bloating the defense budget, eviscerating the already corrupt Environmental Protection Agency, planning to build a useless, expensive wall on the Mexican border, taking immigrant children from their families, giving tax breaks to the nation's richest people, pulling the U.S. out of the Paris climate agreement without even reading it, escalating the bombing raids on defenseless Middle Eastern countries. I'll go on for as long as I can before the security people subdue me. I catch Amy's eye and we share a secret smile, pleased that we're doing something to disrupt the deadly absurdity of twenty-first century America. I know it won't make any difference. I'll just be written off as a left-wing psycho, a potential terrorist. But at least I'll know I didn't just sit back and complain without taking action.

Suddenly there's loud sexy music, and a twenty-something blonde in a bikini bounces onto the stage, starts doing a suggestive dance, loudly chanting: Three-oh-six, three-oh-six, three-oh-six. The crowd picks up the chant: three-oh-six, three-oh-six, three-oh-six, doing sloppy imitations of Bikini Woman's seductive motions. The noise is brutal: three-oh-six, three-oh-six, three-oh-six! The number flashes red on the TV screens in Gothic lettering. I'm not sure what the number means, but Randi leans against me and says: It's the number of electoral votes he got back in 2016. The crowd has to chant the number 306 times to greet the President. Otherwise he won't speak.

He's counting?

Probably his assistants are. I can't imagine him doing it himself.

The sound is hypnotic. Three beats, three body motions, a brief pause, three beats, three body motions, a brief pause, three beats, three body motions, a brief pause: three-oh-six, three-oh-six, three-oh-six! I'm surrounded by people moving their bodies. Randi is trying to resist, arms folded across her chest, looking disgusted. It's hard not to move my own body, even though I know that if I get caught in the rhythm, I'll be submitting to something I shouldn't give in to, an undertow that can't be resisted once you're in its grip. Bikini Girl is straight from a TV game show, one of those blondes that assist the MC by bouncing around the stage without speaking, beaming at the prizes: cars and boats and appliances, trips to boring places.

Just as the last 306 gets chanted, I hear another number: three million votes, three million votes, three million votes! I turn and see a gray-haired guy in the back chanting solo, dressed in fatigues and holding up a Vets for Peace poster. This time I don't need Randi to explain. It's the number of votes the President would have lost by in 2016, except that the nation hasn't outgrown its dated election procedures. Bikini Girl stops dancing, glares, and power-walks to the back of the room. She slaps the Vet for Peace hard, knocks out his dentures, tells him to shut the fuck up. He scrambles on hands and knees to put his teeth back in his mouth. The crowd goes wild. The 306 chant returns full force, starting again from number one, this time with pumping fists and stomping feet.

The President finally walks on stage, a beach ball in a suit he can't quite button. He puts on his meaty, self-satisfied smile in response to loud applause. He lifts his hands, palms facing us, signaling for silence, making a secret sign with his thumb and index finger, the other fingers pointing up to form a crude W, the white supremacy symbol. Suddenly the TV monitors start showing football games again, this time with the sound on, and I assume this is some kind of technical mistake that will get someone fired. But the President starts talking as if the football announcers' voices were parts of his speech. The TVs aren't quite loud enough to drown him out, but they're loud enough to make it hard to follow what he's saying. Of course, it's always hard to follow what he's saying because he's either too dumb to make sense or sees no reason to. But now it's like a deliberate attempt is being made to induce a psychotic condition. Beer and car commercials repeatedly interrupt the game, jingles and voice-over messages that blend seamlessly with the President's words, as if by design. Three minutes later, the TVs blink off and the President goes silent. Thirty seconds later, the TVs and the President start making noise again. This pattern repeats for the next ten minutes. The auditorium lights flash off and on, a strobe effect that makes the President look like he's popping in and out of existence.

Randi says fuck this shit, stands and shouts Hey! raising her hand like a student who wants to make sure she gets called on. He glares at her, snarling that it's not time for questions yet.

Randi snaps: But I won't remember the question later. I have to ask as soon as the question pops into my mind.

The President says: Write it down now, ask it later.

I don't have any paper. My pen has run out of ink.

He leers at her like a sleazy Southern sheriff and says: Sucks to be you, doesn't it?

I notice that Amy is holding up her phone. I assume she's making a video, since Randi looks like she might be staging a disruption similar to the one we've planned. Why not launch two viral videos?

Randi takes a deep breath and says: Here comes the question anyway. Mr. President, when you're making a customer service call and they put you on hold, there's always music playing, really bad music. Who made the decision to play this music? Why is it always so stupid? Why does it always sound like beer commercial music or failed top-40? Why are—

It's an algorithmic decision.

Algorithmic?

Yeah, algorithmic. Al-go-rith-mic.

A decision that no one is making?

Right. We don't need anyone anymore.

Who wrote the algorithm?

No one.

An algorithm wrote the algorithm?

That's one way of putting it.

But someone somewhere at some point must have written something down.

Your thinking is dated. There's no human point of origin. That went out of fashion decades ago. It's cheaper without people. More money for motherfuckers like me. Less money for motherfuckers like you. Got it?

Not really, Mr. Not-My-President. The truth is that some really smart flabby guy with a bad complexion got paid to pick up a number two pencil and put numbers on a piece of lined paper. Or maybe it was graph paper. Or maybe a legal pad, one of the yellow ones with perforations at the top. He wrote things down and crossed things out and had moments of confusion, moments of frustration, then moments of excited understanding. He cleared his throat, scratched his balls, took off his glasses and put them back on, got up to pig out on a pack of Oreos, made himself sick, had to take three Tylenols and sit quietly to refocus himself, then took what he'd written on the page and typed it into a computer. We need to find this guy and others like him. They graduate from top universities. They get paid a lot of money. Without them, motherfuckers like you would be nothing. We need to put these people out of commission.

I'm absolutely stunned. Normally no one talking to the President gets to talk as long as Randi just talked. I'm not at all surprised that he used the word motherfucker, but I'm amazed that she had the balls to repeat it and didn't get silenced and punished.

The President sneers and says: But the fact remains, the flabby guy with the bad complexion didn't decide that when you're on hold on a customer service call, you hear bad music. The algorithm decided. He was just the one writing it down, like someone dancing and speaking in tongues when the Holy Spirit takes over.

That's a fucked up analogy. It's—

The math guy isn't the one who decides on the songs that get played.

They don't really get played. They're just there.

And they always will be. There's no way back to what you think was a better time. It wasn't a better time. Back then, you had to correct your own spelling mistakes.

I didn't make spelling mistakes.

Bullshit.

I really didn't. I always—

Bullshit! We'll get the last four digits of your social security number. We'll use them to dig up your digital past, the only past that exists anymore. There's an algorithm that helps us dig up your shit in no time at all. There's that word again: Algorithm. Al-go-rithm! Like something you can dance to. We'll use it to prove you made spelling mistakes. It's instead of its. Which instead of witch. Here instead of hear. Bare instead of bear. Sale instead of sail. Weight instead of wait. Wail instead of whale. Pie instead of pi. Pale instead of pail. Lay instead of lie. Laid instead of lain or lane. There instead of their and they're. Hair instead of hare. Pear instead of pair. Hi instead of high. By instead of buy. Horrible mistakes you were just too lazy to notice! We'll publish them on your Facebook page. We'll use them to ruin your credit score. We'll put you in a camp for people with subprime credit ratings. Your life will totally suck and it won't get better. Do you really want to continue this conversation?

The President makes the white supremacy sign and the crowd explodes. There are more high fives, pumping fists, and obscene hip movements in the next thirty seconds than there were in all the pro and college football games in 2018.

Randi leans close and whispers in my ear: Do you still want that blow job?

I'm so surprised I don't respond at first, but then I nod eagerly.

She says: Do you have a place?

Yeah. It's only five blocks away.

I'll only do it if we can do it with music on.

What kind of music?

Jazz from the late fifties.

I have a great collection of jazz from the late fifties. But it's all on vinyl and my turntable doesn't work.

No blow job then.

I'm about to suggest an alternative when the President holds up his hands and gives me a dirty look. The TVs go silent and the cop near the fire exit fingers his gun, so I nod and try to look polite. The President glares at Amy and her phone, quickly nods toward Bikini Girl, who sashays across the stage, grabs Amy's phone and smashes it, then clamps her in a headlock and hauls her outside. It happens so fast that I'm not sure how to react. I want to call the police, but I know it would only make things worse. The police work for the man, the beach ball in the suit.

Bikini Girl bounces back through the fire exit, hops onto the stage, does a high-five with the President, who puts on his meaty self-satisfied smile and says: It's time to confront the future, and the future is Space Dot Com, which will ensure that America's dominance in space is never questioned and never threatened, because we know that the best way to prevent conflict is to prepare for victory. It's a big deal, it's a really big deal. Space is the next arena. It's obvious to everyone. It's all about space. Spaaacce: I like the way it melts in my mouth. It's a word I want to keep saying until it doesn't exist anymore.

The President's beefy smile becomes angelic. Joining his hands in front of his paunch, swaying back and forth, gazing at the ceiling as if it were something more than a substitute sky, he says: As emperor of the universe, I will soon be launching specially trained space warriors, intergalactic green berets, prepared to conquer infinity—and beyond! To boldly go where no one has ever gone, to a place that won't exist until it's ours. For those who think they can harm the United States—to challenge us in the ultimate high ground of celestial combat—it's going to be a whole different ball game, and they won't even get to first base. Our future is one big slam dunk after another. Everyone else will have to run for cover.

He pauses to let the syllables plant themselves in everyone's brain. Then he smiles like he's just about to consume a family size pack of double stuff golden Oreo cream sandwiches. It's not the meaty self-satisfied smile he flashed when the speech began. It's the smile of someone whose teeth are getting sharper by the second. He finally says: If I say that the one percent won't pay any taxes, the crowd of mostly working class people goes wild. If I make the W sign, the crowd goes wild.

I know there's no time to lose. Within a few seconds, the crowd will erupt again. I'm on my feet. I take a deep breath. But now that Amy's gone and won't be recording my volley of insults, I'm not sure what to do. I freeze in place with my mouth half open. The President looks at me like I'm a tree that he needs to chop down. I try to look like I'm not a tree, that there aren't any trees anymore. I finally manage to say: Can anyone here tell me what question I'm asking?

The President tries to look like an angry turtle. He points at me and shouts: Silence that man! Fold him in half like a stick of Juicy Fruit gum. Or no, not Juicy Fruit, Spearmint. Or no, not Spearmint, Doublemint. Or no, not Doublemint, Beechnut. Or no, not Beechnut, Wintergreen. Or no, not Wintergreen, Bazooka Joe's. Yeah, Bazooka Joe's! The kind with the cute little comics inside. Or no, not gum, that's a thing of the past. We need something you can eat. Fold him in half like a slab of uncooked bacon. Is there anyone here who doesn't like eating whole packs of uncooked bacon?

Everyone looks amazed by the President's burst of inspiration, too stunned to react when I push my way to the aisle and dart into the bathroom. I know I've only got seconds to make my escape. I stand on a toilet and squeeze out through the window, then rush down the alleyway into the street of pedestrians. I try to look like a normal guy doing normal things. I walk like it's just another night and I'm out for a stroll. I yawn and smile and stroke my chin and look at my watch and put my hands in my pockets, pausing every few minutes to study the merchandise in the shopfronts. It feels like I should be pursued by huge unshaven guys with guns and mirror shades, but when I look back I just see regular people. I keep walking, wondering about Amy, but also wondering why the

President let Randi talk so long and bluntly challenge him. Normally, he only allows you to get half-way through a sentence, then loudly talks over you, changing the subject. He gets mad if you try to return to what you were saying, cutting you off again quickly. So it's odd that he didn't cut Randi off right away. Then it occurs to me: He probably let her talk because he liked the way she looked, the curves her body made in her form fitting outfit. The President's misogyny is well known, one of the media's favorite topics. Now I've seen it in action, but in a surprisingly subtle way.

Across the street, a group of maybe ten people, laughing and playfully pushing each other and talking loudly, apparently drunk, stops in front of a brownstone. One of them opens the door and they stumble inside. They're too drunk to notice or care when I join their party. I figure the President's hit men won't think of searching a private home. Inside, we fill the two front rooms with loud conversation. Soon I'm sitting on a blue couch between two women, who talk to me like they know me well, repeatedly calling me Bart, or maybe Bret. Apparently Bart or Bret used to work at the city zoo, but quit a few months ago because he couldn't stand seeing animals in cages any longer. Now he's part of a mystical cult whose arcane ceremonies involve the spirits of dead animals—crows and wolves and dolphins are mentioned repeatedly, and represent higher forms of intelligence. One of the women is tall and slender and has a necklace of teeth. The other woman has wavy blonde hair and a long iridescent gown. The shifts in color begin to have a strange hypnotic effect. Soon I feel like I've been here for days, or that I grew up in this brownstone, and it's my job to keep it in good condition. This responsibility soon becomes the main topic of conversation. Two men, who suddenly don't seem drunk at all, start talking about renovations, inexpensive ways of making my brownstone as good as new. Then we're discussing budgets and building materials. The iridescent woman, who gets called Nancy, says that her cousin can get special custom work done for almost nothing, since he knows the right people. Everyone at the party agrees that it's crucial to know the right people. I'm feeling elated. Everything seems possible. I start talking to the construction guys, making definite plans, sharing contact information. In the background, Nancy and the necklace woman are whispering, with an urgency that makes it seem that they were waiting for me to leave so they could have a real conversation.

Nancy says: So anyway, Jackie, here's how it works. All you have to do is get him to say his name backwards. Then he'll vanish into the Phantom Zone.

Jackie says: That's it? Really?

Yeah, that's all it takes.

But what if he's got a name you can't say backwards. Like Smith or Brown.

It doesn't have to be his exact name, letter by letter. Even if it sounds like his name backwards, or has a syllable that sounds like his name backwards, it'll send him into the Phantom Zone.

So, let's say his name is Rat. Tar is rat backwards. So if you get him to say guitar or retarded, he'll vanish into the Phantom Zone?

Yeah.

I don't get it. Guitar and retarded are common words and he's probably said them many times throughout his life. So why hasn't he already disappeared?

I was confused about that too, at first. But it turns out the answer is simple. It's the act of *getting* him to say it, *tricking* him into saying it, that makes him disappear.

I still don't get it.

It's not about getting it. We're talking about magic, not logic. It's not scientific, not algorithmic. Neither is the Phantom Zone. It's not part of our scientific universe.

Then what is it?

It's whatever doesn't exist anymore, or never did or never will.

He'll vanish without a trace?

Without a trace. No one will even remember that he existed.

Even I won't remember?

You'll remember, since you'll be the one who got rid of him. But no one else will.

I look over at them, and when they see me looking they shut up and smile politely. I realize that they're not talking about the President. The person they're planning to eliminate might be a boss or spouse or boyfriend. But it's hard not to think about the President when magic is being discussed. Normally, I would dismiss magic as being a show biz activity, tricks that certain people learn to perform on stage. But I'm thinking about it now as a way of understanding how the President got here, and how to get rid of him. In a way, it's perfect. If people were thinking logically, the President would just be another spoiled blowhard who needs to get his ass kicked. But through the crudest forms of media magic, he fooled millions of people into voting for him. So maybe the way to get rid of him would be through a magical action.

I want to ask Nancy where she found out about the Phantom Zone. Maybe she's a witch of some kind, and has a network of supernatural connections and allies, just like Bret or Bart supposedly does. But the construction guys are talking to me earnestly, trying to share important information, and I don't want to be rude by seeming distracted. I meet their eyes and crease my brow and nod every fifteen seconds.

Jackie says: It sounds like something from a comic book.

Nancy says: You want to get rid of him, right? I mean, you've been living with him for years, and he's the worst boyfriend ever.

That's for sure. I've got to get rid of him, but he won't let me break up with him. You remember how violent he got the last time I tried to leave.

So what have you got to lose? Give it a try. Get him to say his name backwards. His name is Lee? So get him to say common words like steal, feel, real, or kneel. Like if Lee were the President, you could get him to start promoting his best-selling book, *The Art of the Deal.*

Jackie's about to say something else. But in the next room a TV comes on, and I can hear the President's voice. It's loud and belligerent, mentioning Iran and Venezuela. They're identified as threats to our national security, obstacles to Democracy, which means that we might need to start bombing them, a prospect that leads to maniacal cheering and shouting from the televised crowd. They're going wild, jumping up and down at the thought of Iran and Venezuela getting slaughtered. I feel sorry that I left

Randi there by herself. Then I think of Amy, who might be in the Phantom Zone at this point. I wonder if there's any way to bring people back, some kind of verbal magic. Then I realize that it might be harder to bring her back if she's not in the Phantom Zone and just in custody somewhere, since magic words won't work and I'll have to hire lawyers, then resign myself to years of expensive bullshit.

Turn that shit off, Nancy yells. One of the construction guys starts fumbling with the remote, thrusting it at the picture tube, but nothing happens.

Jackie says: Haven't you heard? It's now illegal to turn off TV sets when the President is speaking. The off button on the remote won't work.

One of the men nods: Yeah, you're right Jackie, and I've heard that if you turn it off by unplugging it, you get fined and put on a list.

I say: We're all probably on lists of some kind anyway.

Nancy says: So I'm never turning on my TV again.

Jackie says: I think they can turn themselves on.

A man in front of the TV nods and points to the screen: This one just did.

Another man says: Are you allowed to turn down the volume and do something else?

The guy with the remote says: I've been trying to. But it seems to be stuck on high volume, just like the President himself.

I say: Once the TV's on, can they tell if you're really watching?

Nancy says: They? Who's *they*?

I say: Whoever it is that wants to know what you're doing. The ones who write and use algorithms to blow up your phone with ads.

She says: Yeah, but who *are* they? What good does it do them to know what you're doing? What kind of person would want a job like that?

Jackie says: Remember the nerd from your high school calculus class, the one who went to MIT or Caltech and got recruited by Apple or Microsoft? He's the kind of person who wants a job like that. He gets more money in a year than you and I make in a lifetime.

Nancy shakes her head and says: But how can they tell if you're watching and if you're really paying attention? I mean, can't you just pretend to pay attention?

I say: Sure, but I bet that within a year you'll have to *prove* you were paying attention.

Nancy says: How? What would count as proof?

A man says: They'll make you take notes and turn in the notes at the end of each day or week or month or whatever.

Jackie says: And people won't resist because the whole process of collecting and checking the notes will create new jobs, and studies will appear showing that the economy has never been better.

Nancy says: Yeah, but the TV enforcement workers will probably only get minimum wage. And no health benefits or vacation time. Think of the security clearance those jobs will require.

There's a knock at the door. I want to think it's people joining the party, but I'm pretty sure it means danger, guys with guns and mirror shades. I know it's time to leave. I find the bathroom and slip out through the window into an alley, then move carefully onto a side street. I walk for maybe ten minutes, past rows of brownstones that look like the one I just left. Again, I control myself carefully, making sure I don't look like someone being chased by dangerous people. I'm becoming convinced that if you act like you're not being chased, then you're not being chased.

I walk onto a larger, commercial street, back toward the rally, toward the confrontation I tried to run away from. TVs broadcast the President's beach ball face from every shop. He's like some phantom presence haunting the unreality that's created him, as if we were all in the Phantom Zone already, a place where things no longer exist, a place where we can't remember what it meant for things to exist. I look away but keep coming back to the fat face in the shopfronts. I can't hear what he's saying, since the sound is trapped behind the windows, and for all I know the sound might not be on. But there's no need to know what he's saying, since he's not saying anything. He's just bellowing, and the camera repeatedly shifts to the audience jumping up and down like people on daytime game shows. I can see Don't Tread on Me in the tenth row making the white supremacy sign, and two seats to his left Randi is glaring, like someone who wants to flip someone off but knows it might be dangerous. I keep walking, watching the depth of the street reflected in the shopfront glass, watching for the President's hit men, listening for footsteps approaching behind me. But there's nothing. Apparently I've given them the slip. Then I see the large brick structure, the school auditorium, and the noise and light of the rally bursting through the open front door.

When I enter the President is so caught up in the noise he's making that he doesn't seem to notice me. The TVs are going berserk. The word TOUCHDOWN! flashes on and off in red Gothic lettering. I sit back down beside Randi.

She whispers: Where were you?

It's hard to explain.

Why did you come back?

I still want a blow job.

I already told you: No blow job without the right music.

I lie: I got my old stereo system out of my basement while I was home. It still works. We can listen to my jazz collection.

Cool. Let's go.

I still have to do what I came here to do. That's why I came back.

You just said you came back because you still want a blow job.

Multiple motivations. I'm a complex person.

Aren't we all?

No. Just look at who's here with us.

You really think they're all simpletons?

They might as well be.

Really?

I wonder if she's trying to tell me that these people aren't the Tea Party morons they appear to be. But I'm prepared to tell her that I don't care if they cheer for their kids at little league baseball games or dress up as Santa Claus at Christmas parties or take their kids to Sunday School or serve on the PTA or put their kids in Boy Scouts or Girl Scouts or make sure they get good grades or take them on hunting and fishing trips or shopping sprees. I don't care how many so-called redeeming qualities they might have. They're here supporting an oligarchic thug who's making a severely compromised capitalist superpower even more fucked up than it was four years ago. There's no excusing their support for a tyrant.

I know I should probably cut my losses. It's too dangerous to shout insults in a situation like this. If the mob gets violent, no one will stop them from tearing me to pieces. In fact, the security people will probably be pleased that the mob is doing their job for them. But I'm still convinced that I can rely on the element of surprise. When I tell the President what a dangerous monster he is, everyone will be too shocked to react at first, and I already know I can escape once I'm out on the street, since I've already done so.

But then I remember that Amy is gone, and without the viral video she was planning, a crucial part of the project will be missing. It's true that the room is filled with TV cameras recording everything, but they're all focused on the President, and Amy was planning to make my subversive tirade the center of attention, knowing it would reach millions of people on the Net, not reduced to a one-minute clip on the network news. We were counting on copycat responses, thousands of people assaulting the President with vicious insults everywhere he went, making viral videos that would take up huge amounts of virtual space.

I half turn to Randi and whisper: I need a favor.

She whispers: Another one? It's not enough that I'll be giving you a blow job?

It's more than enough. But I need you to take my phone and make a video.

Of what?

You'll see.

I slide the phone slowly out of my pocket. Concealing it in the palm of my hand, I slip it into her hand.

She whispers: Right now?

Right now.

I stand. I start to speak. But the President makes the white supremacy sign and the crowd explodes. Don't Tread on Me leans back and beats his chest and yells like Tarzan. Bikini Woman hops back onstage and starts doing jumping jacks. Randi Castle drops my phone, and I hear the screen crack. She looks at me with a stunned expression, the same face I saw when I asked her for a blow job. She looks like a combination of Nancy and Jackie, and I remember what they said about the Phantom Zone, which sounded ridiculous. But now I'm so disgusted I'll try anything. I need to get the President to say Part, the reverse of his name: Trap. It shouldn't be too hard. Part is a common word.

I wait fifteen minutes for the crowd to get quiet enough. Then I shout: Mr. President, What part of this sentence am I leaving out? He bellows back: The second part comes before the first. But the second part doesn't exist yet. He pops out of existence. The crowd stands there, not sure what to think or do next, not sure if they should be disturbed or entertained by what looks like a magic trick. There's a heap of orange dust beside the podium.

I know I've got no time to lose. I've got to make them start cheering again, so they don't connect me with the President's disappearance. I rush to the aisle and up to the podium, give Bikini Girl a high five, and make the victory sign. They think it's the white supremacy sign. They cheer wildly. I know that by the time the noise dies down, they won't even know who the President was, or that he existed at all.

Robert Boucheron

The Streckfuss-Hamadi Algorithm

Let us assume that A is a young man, college-educated, employed full-time with benefits by a corporation in a field such as market research. For convenience, we will refer to A as "Abe." This shortened version of the name Abraham carries no ethnic connotation, nor does it imply anything about his height, long legs, lean angularity, raven hair, or marked facial features. We may note, however, that Abe is personable, easy-going, smart, and athletic. Abe likes dogs and cats, and he is good with children. He has a sense of humor. Most important for this exercise, Abe is single.

Let us further assume that B is a young woman whose age, university education, white-collar job in emerging market development, taxable income, and physical traits are nearly identical to those of Abe. For convenience, we will call her "Beth." Again this arbitrary syllable, which could be short for Bethany or Elizabeth, implies nothing about her racial background, height, slender figure, muscle tone, lustrous black hair, or remarkably mobile face. Like Abe, Beth is socially aware, relaxed in company, and intelligent. Beth does well with animals and children. She laughs easily. And it is crucial to observe, Beth is single.

While Abe and Beth did not grow up in the same neighborhood, or even live in the same city during their formative years, the similarity of their socio-economic profile ensures that they have much in common. Both, for example, lived in a detached, single-family house for most or all of their childhood, and both spent a good portion of that childhood strapped in the back seat of a private automobile being driven somewhere by a parent. Both expect to live a long and healthy life. Having known happiness, both anticipate a happy future.

In the matter of preferences and habits, it is uncanny how much Beth and Abe are alike. Both enjoy chocolate ice cream, for example. Both always put on the left shoe first. The list could be extended. Yet we must bear in mind that the list does not represent *shared experience*. The habits of Abe which recall those of Beth, and vice versa, do not result from imitation, to take one possible avenue of influence. Rather, the many ways in which Abe and Beth resemble each other should be ascribed to *pure coincidence*.

On meeting each other for the first time at a casual get-together sponsored by a local business enterprise, Beth and Abe are struck by the convergence of their independent and *up to this moment* mutually unknown existence. While each clings to a serving of an alcoholic beverage—a bottle of beer in the hand of Abe and a glass of white wine in the hand of Beth—they continue to chat for over an hour without feeling a need to refresh their drinks or check their messages.

We know that Abe and Beth currently inhabit a North American city that is not particularly attractive to their demographic. Nothing like San Francisco or New York. Opportunities for dating are limited in this otherwise livable and friendly urban environment, which might be in the Great Plains or the Midwest. Moreover, since moving here a year ago, neither Beth nor Abe has made much of an effort to get out and mingle. They take their jobs seriously, their work schedules are demanding, and they often find at the end of the day the amount of surplus energy available for leisure activity is small. It is a lucky chance, therefore, that they both decided to attend this social function, which to be honest did not sound all that appealing when they heard about it.

As the event winds down and the crowd thins, people leave in pairs or small groups, perhaps to catch a bite to eat in the vicinity. Peripherally aware that time is up, Beth and Abe face a challenge. How to objectify this experience? Each came here alone, though both have a wide circle of friends with whom they occasionally socialize. And each has no pressing engagement to which he or she must hurry after this one is done. Given the fortuitous nature of the encounter, nothing will be lost if they leave separately, perhaps never to see one another again.

On the other hand, Abe and Beth know that data in the field of marketing confirm the theory of random motion in physics. Chance plays a major role in determining the path of a subsequent chain of causation, the so-called butterfly effect. How best can they analyze the current problem, identify the variables, and predict the outcome?

It ought to be clear from the information presented up to this point that Beth and Abe, despite a difference in gender which is far from negligible, are as nearly equal as two persons who were not born identical twins can be. Reverting to a quasi-mathematical notation, let us therefore set down the statement:

$$A = B$$

From this simple and culturally neutral proposition, two corollaries are immediately apparent. The first is a certain *reciprocity* in the relationship of A and B, which can also be expressed as a property of *mirror-imaging*. We can most easily see this by reversing the order of the elements:

$$B = A$$

The second corollary is no less true, but perhaps more interesting. Before we can state it, however, we ought to review a few facts. We do not know the intrinsic measure or *absolute value* of A or B, only that one is the same as the other. That value could be large or small, odd or even, positive or negative, a whole number or a fraction, or even an irrational number. Our inquiry does not extend to an estimate of this value, nor do we attach any significance to it. Likewise, we cannot fathom what A and B themselves think they are worth. What we can do is state the obvious:

$$A - B = 0$$

Reverse the order of the elements, and we obtain the equally true statement:

$$B - A = 0$$

In other words, the subtraction of one element from the other yields the empty set, or null. To restate this equation in a more humanistic form, we can say that B minus A equals zero. And if the evening proceeds in the direction it is currently trending, either

Beth or Abe might *think* or *say* something along these lines, such as: "Without you I am nothing."

Before we allow this train of thought to rush headlong to annihilation, let us look at another proposition, one that may lead to a more fruitful discussion, namely:

$$A + B = C$$

To repeat what was said earlier, we do not know what A or B represents in any measurable domain, such as intelligence quotient, grade point average, SAT scores, number of followers as counted by mainstream social media, or medical history. Both appear to be in excellent health. We cannot score their personal satisfaction via the Streckfuss-Hamadi algorithm. But if we can imagine their quantitative or qualitative difference, we can just as well imagine their sum. Add B to A, or A to B, and the result is C.

What is this mysterious C? Where does it come from? It seems to spring from the void, trailing a whiff of ozone. What can we say about C that is not silly and tautological but will contribute to a sound analysis of the problem that Abe and Beth must urgently solve?

Now, it is all too tempting to assign a value of 1 to A and B, so that the equation will read:

$$1 + 1 = 2$$

Unfortunately, this banal statement of singularity and duality tells us nothing we did not already know. In fact, it tends to obscure the real sense of newness that Beth and Abe instinctively feel.

When we consult ancient texts that address this issue, what we find suggests that the value of C is 1. In the biblical book of Genesis, for example, we read: "they shall be one flesh." The fable advanced by Aristophanes in the *Symposium* of Plato, while facetious, makes much the same point by saying that lovers are two halves of what was once a spherical whole. We may express this proposition thus. Since $A = B$, $A + B = 2A = 2B$.

And since A + B = C, 2A = C = 2B. Divide each element by 2, and in Plato's terms:

$$A = \tfrac{1}{2} C = B$$

Beth is frankly impressed that Abe remembers this stuff from college. For his part, Abe is impressed as he watches Beth write equations with a wet finger on a tabletop. By now, the room is quiet. Everyone else has gone home or, as we earlier postulated, to one of several restaurants nearby that feature cuisines from around the world.

Beth took an introductory course in philosophy, but it was dry and dull. They learned about logic and linguistics, uncertainty and incompatibility, but they never got around to the issues she was interested in, the really juicy questions.

Abe can totally relate. He took a survey course in the great philosophers, but it was a lot of names and dates and questions that no one cares about today.

Their eyes meet. By this time of night, each has usually eaten a sensible if hastily prepared meal at home, often while watching a televised news program. Freed from this routine, light-headed from low blood sugar and one twelve-ounce drink containing alcohol, they are hungry. At precisely the same moment, both young people blurt precisely the same words.

"Would you like to have dinner with me?"

Cassandra Passarelli

Fifty-One Rolls

Becoming aware of the day without residual dream memory, Ensa comes slowly onto her knees and sits back on her heels, elongates her spine, stretching her fingertips onto the rug beyond her mattress. She pees, hovering over the icy toilet seat. And puts water on the gas to boil. She prepares half a cantaloupe, a pomegranate, a pear. Spreads butter on a roll. She eats slowly. Being on the fringes can bring you into the core of life.

Pappus called this place the focus. Manaechmus did the earliest work on conic sections. But his theories didn't stand up to later discoveries. Knowledge is this, a temporary hypothesis, fragile and subject to revision. Archimedes explored the method of exhaustion. Apollonius gave the parabola, arms reaching to infinity, its nomenclature. And Galileo had stuff to say about acceleration and the gravity of parabolas.

The sash windows frame her view. The building opposite, almost identical to hers, is swathes of red brick, white pointing, black lead pipes. The chimney stacks sit atop the crest of the seal-grey slates, frosted white with crystals, six pots apiece. The sky is a solid slab of Absolute Grey marble. Across the juniper-green metal railings Tibetan flags flutter. Lavender, ivy, heather and marigolds brush the window sill. The occasional seagull, pigeon or thrush camber before the granite backdrop; birds and flags apart, the scene is static.

From this Ensa's life is stitched. On the windowsill a clay pot contains three orchids, trailing wilting ivory flowers of mournful elegance. Self-preservation is an expression of distress; Nietzsche was quite right about that, but it's not power that's the life force it's simply change. Youth, convinced of its eternity, stays ignorant of decay's immanence. But she's past that bend, beyond the axis of symmetry, on the downward limb, a whole different ball of wax. Perhaps her trajectory is spiralling through a cross-section of a three-dimensional dome. Or she will have to discover it anew like Schatz's oloids or Hirsch's sphericons. Today she nurses the benediction that she will forget the self.

She takes down a stainless steel bowl and empties a kilo and half of brown flour into it. Grinds sea salt, a pinch of Muscovado, a small hill of yeast, a slug of sunflower oil, water from the tap. She blends the ingredients with her right hand, left anchoring the bowl as dough forms. She rolls out three ropes on the Formica, chops them into discs and moulds each into a sphere, arranging them on greased trays.

While the first batch bakes, she showers. The top rack browns fastest and she throws the rolls into a paper bag and puts the next tray in. She dresses; cords, green long-sleeved T, cotton sweater, wool cardigan. She rubs cream into her face and looks at it. When she's awake, like this, it is beautiful, the complexion clear, the eyes alive, the features fine. When she isn't, she barely recognises the dull-eyed stranger in the mirror. There is no way to level this dichotomy. Without vertices or vortexes, no trajectory.

Wrapping a scarf around her neck, pulling on fingerless gloves, she grabs her front door key and slips a fiver in her back pocket. With fifty-one rolls under one arm, and some old Wellingtons under the other, she steps out into the gelid Christmas morning. Blackbirds have dug up the bulbs she planted yesterday. She stops to sweep up the scattered earth.

Martlett Court is possibly at its most lovely in full mid-winter frore. The steamy lit windows on the walkways seem cosier than in other seasons. The branches of the mountain ash are bare; their scarlet berries scattered and smashed on the paving stones. The streets are preternaturally quiet. The familiar dispossessed that sleep opposite the derelict Bow Street Police Station are not there, though a couple of their homes are folded and leant against the wall. The Royal Opera House's revolving doors are still. Not a laptop glows in a single cafe. A few displaced tourists stray into the piazza, deserted of shoppers on smartphones or entertainers on soapboxes. Fowler's uncluttered neo-classical façade is accentuated by the desolation. Covent Garden station's metal accordion gates are drawn. Marks and Spencer is dark.

The man in Amorino's doorway sleeps, so she does not disturb him. In Jones Bootmaker's recessed entrance is a cardboard screen, but nobody's behind it. The rolls warm her body through her coat and she shifts them under the other arm. Taking a left down Saint Martin's Lane toward Trafalgar Square two squatters are leaning against a wall. The woman is not more than twenty; her fine features pierced and framed by dreadlocks, her long shirt and leggings thin against the wind. He is tall, shaved temples crown Slavic features, hazel epicanthic eyes and a nose, impaled by a long screw. Ensa asks them where the squat is.

'We've been evicted,' they answer. His is a mellow Brummie accent while hers is RP.

'Eight o' clock this morning,' he adds.

'They sent bailiffs in,' she nods at the gate where a stocky man in a bullet-proof vest shifts from one foot to another.

'The bailiffs had no papers, the cops kicked us out, illegal-like. It was me who called them in the first place.'

'All our stuff is in there.'

'The judge ruled we could stay. We could go back in, the judge said, but we'd have to hire our own bailiff.'

'We don't even have a blanket.' She starts rolling-up.

'The company that owns it, Greencap something-or-other, is registered in Jersey. They filed accounts last year; valued themselves at nine quid. Five carpeted storeys in central London with a bathroom and all! You should see the view from up there. Nine quid!'

'We sat on the balcony for eight hours yesterday.'

'Ten, Mouse,' he says.

'Ten. It was rented out to the Royal Bank of Scotland,' Mouse adds, falling into a PR patter after three days on national TV. 'Who were bailed out by the government, which means taxpayers money: we're only taking back what's ours.'

'More than thirty thousand homes in London are empty. Not to mention offices like these.'

'I brought some bread for the lunch,' says Ensa.

'The others are just getting some tables; we'll be up and running in an hour,' says Mouse.

Ensa continues walking. The first rough sleeper she comes across has put his piece of cardboard at right angles to the pavement. He is a large, restless black man under a blanket that's too short for him. He pulls his blanket up to his chin, tries to catch the other end with his toe and pull it down over his feet. The moment his feet are covered he yanks it up again, repeating the sequence, in serial reiteration. She hasn't the courage to disturb him.

On Garrick Street two men approach, the one with a twisted ankle, limping badly. They are bearded, carrying their belongings and zip-locked packed lunches and trailing sleeping bags. They hesitate at her offer so she tips the open bag so they can see in, smell the bread. They speak to each other in an Eastern European language. The older man's dirt-filled creases are so deep he could be one of Rembrandt's potato-eaters. He puts his hand in and takes one roll though she gestures he should take another. The younger also takes just one.

On Endell Street, three Scousers have bedded down beneath the overhang of Nuffield's brown-brick seventies building, where the swimming pool extractor is pumping out a warm chlorine haze. A young, fair-haired girl with freckles and clear blue eyes sits between two guys.

'I need these two. First, because I'm one of the few women out here. Second, because I can't handle the lights; I'm epileptic.'

'What size shoe are you?' asks Ensa.

'Five and a half,' says the girl.

'My kid's Wellingtons, they're as good as new, could you use them?'

'Cheers!'

'Have a good Christmas,' they call.

Further down Endell Street two Glaswegians with sanguine complexions prop up the doorway of the sports centre. They raise their Tenants to her.

'Our hands aren't clean.' Ensa shrugs.

'God bless you,' calls the fatter one and the other: 'Thank you, darling.'

They call again, waving goodbye, even as she turns the corner into Shorts Gardens. She makes her way through the back streets to High Holborn, scanning the pavement to differentiate between refuse bags and human beings. Outside the Aldwych Theatre a bald man wearing glasses is lying on his belly, on a blanket, stirring a small brown vial with a stick with one hand and holding a paperback in the other.

'No, thank you, my dear, not hungry. Very kind.'

The other side of the crescent a young man has occupied a double doorway and is spreading out all his donations on a blanket below a tree decorated with tinsel and bows.

'Too much food, look,' he shows her, He opens a bag packed with instant noodles, cakes and biscuits.

'Where is everyone?'

'Over at Crisis. I don't go though, no, not me. You might find some of us along the Strand.' His eyes are hyacinth-blue.

There's nobody at the east end, but when she gets to Ryman's there's a guitarist in his sixties, with fine white hair setting up. He looks in the paper bag and shakes his head. A small knot of itinerants by Charing Cross Station take the bread which has dropped to body temperature. Down Villiers Street, she hands one to a plump Pole and on Northumberland Avenue to a freckled man in his sleeping bag who gruffly thanks her.

She swings back up toward Trafalgar Square, filling with tourists. Outside the old RBS building, a couple of tables are out with sandwiches and salads, sweets and beers. Several Love Activists, uniform in their non-conformity, shaved and dreadlocked, are hanging out. They wear brightly coloured, layered, comfortable old clothes and boots that have walked places. A muzzled pitbull called Zeus barges into everyone.

A ditzy, chapped-skinned woman who introduces herself as Phaedra starts talking to her. She lives on a barge in Richmond with ten others, 'escaping the madness' she says, between bits of a crayfish sandwich that 'might be a bit dodgy.'

'Did you ever read Rousseau's 'Discourse on Inequality'?' she asks. 'He said whoever was the first to mark out a piece of ground, claim it as his and found people stupid enough to agree was the founder of civil society.' Ensa smiles. 'And if someone had been smart enough to pull up the stakes or fill in the ditch mankind would have spared a multitude of crimes, wars and murders.'

'Inarguably.'

'You are lost, says Rousseau, if you forget the fruits are everyone's and the earth no-one's.'

'Fuck, I'm buying a copy.'

She leaves the remaining half bag of rolls with the rest of the food. As she walks 'home' she considers the word; with its Indo-European root in *kei*, to settle down. Settling. What does that mean? Allowing sediment to sink to the bottom. Getting stuck in the parabola's trough. She remembers previous homes that ended up scrambled or undone. The house her parents were evicted from when she was already an absent teenager. The council flat she abandoned, after ten years, when she left the boyfriend it belonged to. Her first house, left when she divorced the husband she bought it with. The temporary dwellings that ended with evictions, no water or a murder on the doorstep. Those all too familiar scenarios; arguments that led to throwing-out, walking-out or severance. She'd been lucky; her nights in the street have been few.

Her current abode is one room with oiled oak floors, a sash window at each end and all she and her daughter need within four walls. Their sanctuary for more than two years, longer than she has stayed in any one place for almost twenty. Her mother had talked her into this flat. She was afraid it would tie her down; make a citizen and hypocrite of her. But now she has stepped from wandering into domesticity. From drifter to taxpayer. From outsider into urban dweller. There are implications.

She had done everything to let in light. Discarding the furniture which filled it to the brim, replacing it with rugs, cushions, winding wool around the lamps, painting the walls, a friend had covered the strip light with a stained-glass window. She'd felt unwonted loneliness in that room at first. A deeper, more desperate alienation than she'd ever met before. Inclement weather trapped her in its narrow confines; she cursed as she dried clothes on radiators, fell asleep to the whir of the washing machine or put on a coat reeking of last night's dinner. When folk slept over they were like puppies in a basket, clambering over each other.

As she presses her fob to the scanner, she thinks of Jeff at number four, who'd died last year, telling her about walkways filled with offspring who didn't know their own mothers. She passes Scheherazade's door, the kindly insomniac. Next to her lives Carol-Anne, a gentle-hearted spinster. Beside her, the eccentric Columbian, Graciela, who tutors her kid in maths out of the goodness of her heart. In number one are the Scotswoman, Janet, and her grandson, Tyler, with his warm, easy prattle.

She walks the first flight of stairs. On this level lives the thespian Shirley with her theatrical voice, who invited them to her birthday party on a Thames barge. And the silent, stocky guy, who'd pumped up her bike tyre when it was flat. Next to him, her big-hearted black neighbours, Justin and Anna, who'd kissed her in Saint Paul's after the midnight mass last night.

On the second floor lives the bald, toothless set designer, Rob, who'd given her daughter his keyboard and kept his dead cat in his fridge till the stench reeked so badly they had to hold their breath on the stairwell. And the powdered Melba, who'd invited them for tea and told them they were precious as her daughter ate every last one of her chocolate-coated biscuits.

She turns up to the third flight where Mergim and Alton live, her kid's Kosovan schoolmates. And Joe, the octogenarian Paddy, who did high kicks whenever he saw her just to prove he could.

At the fourth she passes the crumb strewn entrance of the recluse who sent them a

Christmas card in his Welsh cursive. And her immediate neighbours, two nouveau riche Muscovites, art students, who return in the early hours in luxuriant furs, miniskirts and bling, trailed by noisy Russian men.

She puts her copper key in the silver lock. Each time it turns she doesn't quite believe it. As though she's dreaming someone else's dream, that only Rumi's sleeper could have faith in. She hangs her coat on the peg, unlaces her boots, sashays across the floor and does a little leap and a somersault. Because she's quite possibly the parabola's vertex itself, in motion, arms stretching to infinity. And because that's what she imagines the men sleeping in the stinking alley below would do if they were in her socks.

Dan Moreau

Find X

X and Y got married. They had a son, Z. All the integers at school made fun of him. "You're not even a number," they said. He went home crying. He asked his parents why he was different. "Because you're a variable, honey." "What does that mean?" "It means you can be any number you want." Z stopped crying. "Really?" His parents nodded proudly. His spirits lifted, he returned to school the next day with his head raised high.

A group of popular integers were standing by a locker. As he walked by, they said, "Why do you go to school here? You're not even a number. Why don't you go to school with the other letters?" The popular integers high fived each other.

Z stepped up to them. "I'm not afraid of you. I'm a variable. I can be anything I want to be."

The integers laughed. "Who is this kid? What a weirdo."

Z popped one of the integers in the face, bloodying his nose. Z was suspended from school for three days. His parents were disappointed. When they picked him up, they didn't even say anything. They just drove home in silence.

Z started hanging out with a bad crowd, the exponents and the fractions. The exponents were unpredictable. The fractions were just weird. One night they held up a convenience store. The clerk, who kept a shotgun behind the counter, shot Z in the head. Parts of his brain and skull were scattered all over the store. Of all the numbers he could represent, no one had ever told him he could be nothing.

Matthew James Babcock

Forms: I & II

Forms: I

1. Bigsby, Christopher. *Arthur Miller 1915-1962*. Cambridge: Harvard UP, 2009.

   a.   "Why torment yourself with hellos?" (639).

            Why inflate yourself with bellows?
            Why augment ourselves with fellows?
            Why foment summer with mayflies?
            Why hopscotch herself to Holland?
            Why outsource our souls for solace?
            Why circle bonfires with candles?

2. "1 Corinthians 15:19." *The Holy Bible: Quatercentenary Edition*. Oxford: Oxford UP, 2010.

   a.   "If in this life only we haue hope in Christ, wee are of all men most miserable."

            When with a bath rarely I baste skin in sun, I become for scrawny cannibals quite delectable.

            If in this pond vaguely you see yourself in pain, you stay in this pose so immobile.

            While in yonder topiary nudely she plays lyres of fire, she is for many dudes way desirable.

As around blue rooms sluggishly they drag moods through maroon, they become like drooping roses more purple.

3. Hitler, Adolf. *Mein Kampf.* Translated by Ralph Manheim. Boston: Houghton Mifflin, 1999.

   a. "I had honored my father, but my mother I had loved" (18).

       Thou shalt jostle thy costermonger, but thy viscount thou shalt trounce.

   b. "Hunger was then my faithful bodyguard" (21).

       Arousal is now your rowdy turncoat.

   c. "Austria was then like an old mosaic; the cement, binding the various little stones together, had grown old and begun to crumble" (124).

       Sunset rolls in like a gold Cadillac; the sky, sweeping the abandoned rural drive-in clean, now glows red and returns to splendor.

   d. "Under a whirlwind of drumfire that lasted for weeks, the German front held fast, sometimes forced back a little, then again pushing forward, but never wavering" (191).

       At a barbecue of strangers that summons the cops, the diapered toddler sallies forth, gently shushed down a skosh, once more stumbling sideways, and always babbling.

   e. "The regiment had turned into a few companies: crusted with mud they tottered back, more like ghosts than men" (201).

Our love has soured to a fluent slur: winged with shadows we circle alone, less for movement than memory.

f.   "A few hours later, my eyes had turned into glowing coals; it had grown dark around me" (202).

Beyond the moonless hour, our silences have bellied like goldening thunderheads; they have molded majesty within us.

g.   "Thus cultures and empires collapsed to make place for new formations" (296).

Loose vultures and vampires relapse to suck face with plump seductresses.

h.   "Slowly he makes himself the spokesman of a new era" (314).

Jaggedly bird flight stains June the hues of your private blue.

4. Berry, Chuck. "You Never Can Tell." *From St. Louis to Liverpool*. Chess Records, 1964.

a.   "*C'est la vie* say the old folks, it goes to show you never can tell."

Takie jest życie moan the stoic Poles, it's just a fact some gomers can't spell.

έτσι είναι η ζωή squeak the sleek Greeks, hey yo, your phat beats flay my fontanelle.

Lokho ukuphila croon the Zulus, with hips like ours you hula like hell.

Se on elämää lisp the thin Finns, the flimsy fluff and whimsy sells well.

Tio vivo chant the Esperantists, cram sandwiches with scams, they still smell.

Quod est vitae quote the Romans, it's clear to us you ain't no Philomel.

Sin beatha snarl the bold Celts, buck naked you can fight 'em just as well.

Sore ga jinsei desu joke the Japanese, look American with a little more gel.

Bhawarae bleat the Burmans, my politics, your newest nouvelle.

Así es la vida sigh the Hispanics, her lips of blood, her eyes of the gazelle.

5. Tolstoy, Leo. *A Letter to a Hindu*. Introduction by Mahatma Ghandi. Starling and Black Publications, 2013.

a.   "If only people freed themselves from their beliefs in all kinds of Ormuzds, Brahmas, Sabbaoths, and their incarnation as Krishnas and Christs, from beliefs in Paradises and Hells, in reincarnations and resurrections, from belief in the interference of the Gods in the external affairs of the universe, and above all, if they freed themselves from belief in the infallibility of all the various Vedas, Bibles, Gospels, Tripitakas, Korans, and the like, and also freed themselves from blind belief in a variety of scientific teachings about infinitely small atoms and molecules and in all the infinitely great and infinitely remote worlds, their movements and origin, as well as from faith in the infallibility of the scientific law to which humanity is at present subjected: the historic law, the economic law, the law of struggle and survival, and so on—if people only freed themselves from this terrible accumulation of futile exercises of our lower capacities of mind and memory called the 'Sciences,' and from the innumerable divisions of all sorts of histories, anthropologies, homiletics, bacteriologics, jurisprudences, cosmographies, strategies—their names are legion—and freed themselves from all this harmful, stupefying ballast—the simple law of love, natural to man, accessible to all and solving all questions and perplexities, would of itself become clear and obligatory" (21-22).

When finally citizens sink themselves in their lust for new styles of PEDs, BVDs, IUDs, and their substitution for Conversation and Family, in lust for Donuts and   Droids, for liposuctions and implantations, in lust for the circumference of the Rumors in the scandalous dope of the neighborhood, but below that, when they sink themselves in lust for the availability of all the vapid Dramedies, Tabloids, Infomercials, Updates, Newsfeeds, and so forth, and next sink themselves in syrupy lust for a pittance of soporific ramblings about endlessly long bills and legislation and for all the endlessly gray and endlessly redundant ideals, their blandishments and jingles, as well as in love with the achievability of the political utopia with which viewers are at present obsessed: the stump speech, the legacy speech, the speech of hope and revolution, so what's new?—when citizens finally sink themselves in this audacious agglutination of fantastic fripperies about our deepest drumbeats of bowel and hormone called the 'Dream,' and in the unfathomable Jacuzzi of many strains of fabrications, forgeries, buzzwords, histrionics, tautologies, recrudescences, apathies—their brands are seasonal—and steep themselves in all this flavorless, fattening pomp—the winged song of the will, foreign to consumers, priceless to some and canceling all sales and slogans, can once again become blunt and barren.

Forms: II

1. Tolstoy, Leo. *The Devil and Other Stories*. Translated by Louise and Aylmer Maude, Oxford UP, 2003, p. 235.

    a. "And she scorched him with her smiling eyes."

        For we shambled home in our shoddy shoes.
        And you scoured me with your saline stare.
        But they schooled us in their sultry tones.
        Or he sways her in her somber zone.
        Yet she scribes hymns on a stolen stone.
        So I shave love to the burning bone.

2. Larkin, Philip. *Collected Poems*. Introduction by Anthony Thwaite, Farrar, Straus, and Giroux, 2003.

    a. "All the unhurried day your mind lay open like a drawer of knives" (67).

        For one unburnished breath their faces stay grooved like a scream of rivers.

    b. "Lozenge of love! Medallion of art! O wolves of memory! Immensements!" (144).

        Catapult of cloves! Turban of turbulence! O mimes of mutiny! Iridescences!

    c. "Heat is the echo of your gold" (145).

        Red is the reverb in my revelry.
        Silver is the axis of rotten autumn.
        Salamanders meander black gold through luscious rushes.

3.   Player. "Baby Come Back." *Player*, RSO, 1977.

    a.   "All day long, wearing a mask of false bravado, trying to keep up a smile that hides a tear."

        Six feet tall, schlepping a cask of salsa tomatoes, stretching to cork off a spigot that foams a beer.

        No damn fun, stunning a club of sullen commandos, stumbling to snuff out the smoke that fumes her bower.

        Plump blue plums, brimming with tones of summer nocturnals, plunging to burst on starved grass that yellows the sky.

        Tart orange sun, scorching the slats on white gazebos, waiting to swing like a clapper that cracks a bell.

        Charred black walls, blazing with graffiti from fleet banditti, toppling to fall on a shaman that shelters a seed.

4.   *Tao Te Ching*. Translated by David Hinton, Counterpoint, 2015.

    a.   "Ancient masters of Way, all subtle mystery and dark-enigma vision, they were deep beyond knowing, so deep beyond knowing we can only describe their appearance: perfectly cautious, as if crossing winter streams, and perfectly watchful, as if neighbors threatened; perfectly reserved, as if guests, perfectly expansive, as if ice melting away, and perfectly simple, as if uncarved wood; perfectly empty, as if open valleys, and perfectly shadowy, as if murky water" (56).

Tubby cashier at Foodtown, in cat costume and morning-shift scowl, she slouches still without smiling, so still without smiling I can't fully divine her story: doggedly staring, as if hypnotizing kidney beans, and doggedly single, as if boyfriends backpedaled; doggedly drugged, as if cloned, doggedly raucous, as if vulgarity shaking break room, and doggedly devoted, as if only child; doggedly stolid, as if eroded bone, and doggedly dreamy, as if routinely alone.

Kevin Cocozello

Why I Write 1.0

People ask me why do I write?
      I tell them so I could take the pain away –
so I could break away from the chains and have my everything levitate
      This is how I meditate, and even though the more I write the more I desecrate –
      because if it means one heart stopping for one starting, then that's my better place, that's
how I deregulate
. . . And this is why I write . . .
      so I could resurrect through the mist from my abyss –
for the purpose of giving back to every hopeless kid
I feel like I could fix so many faucets of their drips –
I could calm the tide with my lips, move oceans with a kiss, I could heal the pain of hate and
change every single nation with my bliss
. . . And this is why I write . . .
      because when my soul screams that's when my tears flow –
and when my tears flow, they plummet and soak the earth and that's how my seeds grow
and how my seeds grow is by rising through filth by fire and water, that's how my seeds glow –
and how my seeds glow is my Him, me and His kinfolk
. . . And this is why I write . . .
To change a life by poetic suicide
. . . And this is why I write . . .
To find tragic love by what magic does
. . . And this is why I write . . .
To maintain the pain by growing better days
                And this is why I write
                    This is why I write
                 This is why I'll die

Hannah Kauders

A Pragmatic Analysis of the Subjunctive Mood in a Breakup Letter

I	II
Instances of the Imperative Mood	Instances of the Subjunctive Mood

No soy bueno escribiendo
I'm no good at writing

The speaker states that he is no good at writing.
A lie told to appeal to the positive face of his interlocutor,
who is a writer.

Espero que me perdones [la mala redacción]
I hope you will forgive me [for my poor composition]

A directive speech act. The speaker
introduces the first of many pleas:
forgive me, darling, for
you deserve better
than my words.

La noche que te conocí, tomaste
varias copas de Rioja
y me hablabas tan rápido
The night when I met you, you drank
several glasses of Rioja
and were talking to me so quickly

In the indicative, the speaker describes his memory of their meeting.
He is saying: no hypothetical here.
This is our story.

> ¿Qué es lo que debe haber pasado
> Para que nuestros caminos se crucen?
> *What must have happened*
> *To make our paths cross?*

> The past subjunctive indicates what occurred despite
> all odds, indicates the intervention of chance.
> As in a meeting of souls born of two hemispheres
> in a dive near Fenway Park
> (the path, wrote J.L. Austin,
> is a conceptual metaphor for the trajectory
> of a human life).

Era tan pequeña la posibilidad,
pero de alguna forma sucedió
The possibility was so slight,
and yet it happened

The speaker utilizes the preterite indicative:
it might not have happened,
and yet it did,
a coup de foudre,
and here we are.

Cariño, te pido que no me juzgues por estos días
Darling, I ask that you not judge me for these past few days

Another directive: the speaker hopes that you
will not judge him for his behavior. He is asking
politely, he is not begging, nor mandating, he is using
the term of endearment to attenuate, to recall you to
his affection for you, to ask you to remember.

Me enamoré de ti, [insert name of interlocutor]
De tu castellano andaluz, tu acento de Boston
Tus ojos, tu cabello
I fell in love with you,
With your Andalusian Spanish, your Boston accent
Your eyes, your hair

that he loved you, not just anyone but you—
your eyes, your hair, your Southern-Spanish Spanish,
your flat Brahmin vowels, You

Quiero que te acuerdes de lo mucho que te quiero
I ask that you remember how much I love you

I love you, indicative mood. I ask, subjunctive mood,
that you remember it.

Te prometo que las cosas no van a seguir así

I promise that things will be different

In the Spanish, commissive speech acts
require the indicative mood. To promise is not
speculative, not contingent. To promise is to declare:
it will be this way because I say so,
there will be no more long nights,
there will be only rambling mornings of searching the
sheets for each other's faces, of Coltrane on the radio, of
our bodies tied into a single languageless knot.

Te ruego que te quedes sólo un día más
all this if you just stay just one more day

Sé que te he herido
Fui intolerante, impaciente
The indicative is used as an admission of guilt:
I was intolerant, I was impatient
My indicative has imposed its reality over this romance
But now I make my appeal:

Ahora yo te pido que me des una oportunidad más
para probarte que podamos construir un futuro
juntos, para enmendar mis errores,
para quererte
if that you would let me love you, if that you
would build your world with me inside of it, if that if that
if you'd only

¿Te acuerdas de la primera noche, mi amor?
Llegué a Boston ese invierno tan frío para encontrarte con un bolso
gigante afuera de mi puerta, valiente
y lista para quererme.

remember the first night, my love.
The speaker appeals to the positive self-image of his interlocutor,
calling her brave. Because
this is what happened:
it was no dream,
no speculation:
it was January, your face was chapped,
and you were brave—brave to wield your suitcase
on the threshold between one life and another,

not knowing what the mood would be of his response
or in what language he would greet you

Harold Jaffe

Dada

Imagine Dada, birthed during the massive senseless murdering of World War 1, as an in-your-face senselessness.

A special kind of nothing.

Nothing as anti-"meaning," as excrement, as the vomit of endless public speechifying.

There are other nothings.

The vibrating space between two Beethoven chords in his Grosse Fuge.

The unexpected vibrant emptiness of the raked gravel passages in the Ryoan-ji rock garden in Kyoto.

A wise human said that when being begins no-thing matters.

That no-thing erupts silently into the energized matter of Buddhist meditation.

Nihilism is a brutal payback to the prevailing nothing.

Not unrelated, is the nothing of suicide, void in the shape of a razor or noose or 12-gauge aimed at a chest.

A selfie.

Which points to the current ubiquitous nothing culled from Descartes and what passes for lawfulness.

Purportedly it officially commenced with "attempts to solve the *Entscheidungsproblem*."
It is soulless and will not bleed.
If *you* bleed, this Cartesian nothing will avert its gaze.
Dada was aimed at the brain and chest but was not confluent with suicide, especially
before being coopted by the surrealist power-broker Andre Breton.

Engaging characters infected Dada: Hugo Ball, Hans Arp, Kurt Schwitters, Francis
Picabia, Meret Oppenheim, and later, the inimitable duo of Duchamp and Man Ray.

I have a special fondness for the Romanian Jewish Dadaist Tristan Tzara, small and
supple and antic with his monocle and comical posing.
In one of those group photos so common among early artists in every genre, Tzara
always posed in a way that set him apart—raised on someone's shoulders, with his
foot in the air waving his monocle, standing on his head.

I often think of artistic brilliance in pairs: Graham Greene and Max Frisch; Roman
Polanski and Charles Manson; Clarice Lispector and Emily Dickinson; Andrei
Tarkovsky and Robert Bresson; Theodore Kaczynski and Jerzy Kosinski; Goya and
Van Gogh; Brando and Belmondo; Nina Simone and Jeanne Moreau; Kathy Acker
and Anais Nin; Egon Schiele and Otto Dix.

Tristan Tzara is melded in my imagination with Jean-Luc Godard; they never met.

Contributors

Charles Joseph Albert works as a metallurgist, lives with his wife and three sons, and writes poetry and fiction. His work has appeared recently in *Carte Blanche*, *Vallum*, *Write City*, *Amsterdam Quarterly*, and the *Apeiron Review*. His first novel, *The Unsettler*, is currently being released by *SERIAL Magazine*, and his third volume of poetry, *Confession to the Cockroaches and Other Poems*, has just been released by *Dangeray Press*.

Matthew James Babcock teaches composition, creative writing, and literature at BYU-Idaho. Books include *Points of Reference* (Folded Word), *Strange Terrain* (Mad Hat), *Heterodoxologies* (Educe Press), *Four Tales of Troubled Love* (Harvard Square Editions), *Private Fire: Robert Francis's Ecopoetry and Prose* (U of Delaware Press), and *Future Perfect* (forthcoming, Engine Books). Awards include AML Poetry Award, Dorothy Sargent Rosenberg Poetry Award, and Juxtaprose Poetry Award.

S. Bennett's work is published in a variety of venues including *Columbia Journal*, *Indiana Review*, *Los Angeles Review*, *Oxford Magazine*, *Texas Review*, *Tulane Review*, *Wisconsin Review*, and *Paris Transcontinental - Sorbonne (FR)*. He was the founding editor of *THE SOUTHERN ANTHOLOGY* and taught Fiction Writing at UCLA and the University of Louisiana. He currently lives in Florida, sharing the environment with many large iguanas.

Eric Blix is the author of the short story collection, *Physically Alarming Men* (Stephen F. Austin State University Press). His writing has appeared in such journals and anthologies as *Best Small Fictions*, *The Collagist*, *Caketrain*, *The Pinch*, and others. Born and raised in northwestern Minnesota, he currently lives in Salt Lake City, where he studies in the PhD program in creative writing at the University of Utah.

Robert Boucheron is an architect in Charlottesville, Virginia. His stories and essays appear in *Bellingham Review*, *Fiction International*, *London Journal of Fiction*, *Saturday Evening Post*, and online magazines.

Ron Burch's fiction has been published in numerous literary journals including *Mississippi Review*, *New World Writing*, *PANK*, and been nominated for the Pushcart Prize. *Bliss Inc.*, his debut novel, was published by BlazeVOX Books. He lives in Los Angeles.

Kenneth Calhoun has had stories published in *Ploughshares*, *The Paris Review*, *Tin House*, *Ninth Letter*, *New Stories from The South* and *the PEN/O. Henry Prize Collection*, among others. His novel *BLACK MOON* was published in 2014 by Hogarth. "The White Woman" is an excerpt from a novel-in-progress called *CELESTE*. He currently lives in Boston, where he teaches graphic design at Lasell University.

Sophie Calhoun was born in San Diego and raised in Durham, North Carolina. She is a designer and illustrator living in Somerville, Massachusetts. When not dabbling in game design, motion graphics, and interactive art, she's striving to capture the intangible and ambiguous in her illustrations. Her most recent work has focused on relationships between people and their bodies, their memories, and the world around them.

Alex Checkovich is an instructor of "the body in space" at the University of Richmond, where he teaches freshman seminars called "Nature," "Health," and "Technology in American History." His true love is inventing hermit crab essays and Oulipo nonfiction. Work is out or forthcoming with *Territory*, *Passages North*, *PANK*, *Seneca Review*, *Sycamore Review*, *Crab Fat*, and *Badlands*.

Kevin Cocozello is currently incarcerated in Greenhaven Correctional Facility. He is an aspiring writer who is also passionate about working with the youth once released. He has learned deeply from his bad decisions and hopes to inspire the world to be unforgettable. This is his third published prose and first nationwide. Kevin would like to sincerely thank Mr. Jaffe for giving him a chance—especially after the numerous letters he sent annoying him.

Robert James Cross is a Pushcart Prize nominated author. His work has been featured in *pacificREVIEW*, *Fiction International*, and *The Lit Quarterly*. Born in East Los Angeles, raised in Hollywood, living in San Diego. Peculiar forms and unconventional techniques are what drive his writing.

Jaiden Dokken is a 20something from Sequim, WA. She is a writer, ceramicist, drawer, painter, penpal, and cidermaker. Prone to nesting, she loves soup and her people, above all else.

em fowler grew up outside of Baltimore, Maryland. Their work has appeared in online and print publications including *Sycamore Review*, *Occulum Journal*, *Homology Lit Mag*, *Glittermob*, and elsewhere. They are a Chichimec artist living in Kumeyaay territory.

Rosalind Goldsmith lives in Toronto. She has written radio plays for CBC Radio Drama and a play for the Blyth Theatre Festival. Her short stories have appeared in journals in the UK, the USA and Canada, including *Litro UK*, *Filling Station*, *the Blue Nib*, and *the Chiron Review*. She is currently working on a collection of short fiction.

Text Greshan is a poet living in Key Largo.

Kathleen Heil is writer and translator of poetry and prose whose work appears in *The New Yorker*, *FENCE*, *The Threepenny Review*, and many other journals. A recipient of fellowships and awards from the National Endowment for the Arts and the Robert Rauschenberg Foundation, among others, she lives and works in Berlin. More at kathleenheil.net.

Harold Jaffe is the author of 28 volumes of fiction, docufiction, and essays, most recently *Induced Coma, Sacred Outcast, Goosestep, Anti-Twitter,* and *Porn-anti-Porn. BRUT: Writings on Art & Artists* is forthcoming Winter 2020 from Anti-Oedipus.

Hannah Kauders is a writer, translator, and educator based in New York. She is an MFA candidate in Fiction at Columbia University, where she teaches first-year writing.

KKUURRTT is glad you read his thing.

Barbara Lock is a writer, emergency room physician, and currently a graduate student at Sarah Lawrence College, where she is working towards an MFA. Lock graduated from Dartmouth College and Boston University School of Medicine. She has previously published in Best Short Stories from *The Saturday Evening Post* Great American Fiction Contest 2020.

Kon Markogiannis is an experimental photographer-mixed media artist-visual poet-independent researcher with an interest in themes such as memory, mortality, spirituality, the human condition, the exploration of the human psyche and the evolution of consciousness. He currently lives and works in Thessaloniki, Greece.

Stephen-Paul Martin has published many books of fiction, poetry, and nonfiction. He co-directs San Diego State's MFA program.

Ben Miller is the author of *River Bend Chronicle: The Junkification of a Boyhood Idyll amid the Curious Glory of Urban Iowa* (Lookout Books). His prose has been featured in *Best American Essays, Raritan, Yale Review,* and *Antioch Review.* He is the recipient of creative writing fellowships from the National Endowment for the Arts and the Radcliffe Institute for Advanced Study at Harvard University. This work was inspired by the drawings of Dale Williams.

Dan Moreau's fiction has appeared in *Another Chicago Magazine, Shenandoah,* and *Third Coast.* His work has been read live on stage at *Selected Shorts,* and he is the recipient of an Elizabeth George Foundation Grant.

Toby Olson's *Death Sentences* (poetry) just appeared from Shearsman. His 11th novel, *Walking,* will appear from Chatwin Press at the end of November.

Ngozi Oparah is a queer, first-generation Nigerian-American woman. She has her bachelor's in Neuroscience and Philosophy from Duke University and she recently graduated from California College of the Arts with a Master of Fine Art in Creative Writing. She currently works as the Director of Community Programs at StoryCenter in Berkeley, California. Her work has appeared in *Madwomen in the Attic, QXotc,* and *A Velvet Giant.*

Cassandra Passarelli lives with her daughter in Devon, England. She's doing a creative writing PhD on the convergence of Zen and the short story at the University of Exeter. She has published stories in *Question, Ambit, Chicago Quarterly Review, Carolina Quarterly* and five stories in an appropriately named anthology, *Five by Five.* She has also managed a London charity, written theater reviews, set up a children's library foundation in Guatemala, and taught yoga.

Carrie Seidler moved to San Francisco in 2016 after spending 8 years in New York City where she studied improv comedy and sketch writing with the Upright Citizens Brigade. She now teaches high school for formerly incarcerated and historically underserved communities throughout the Bay Area. A recent graduate of the SFSU MFA program in fiction, Carrie is proud to share this chapter from her upcoming novel, *Czech Glory Hole Massacre*.

Marilyn Stablein is a poet, essayist, fiction writer and artist. Recent books include *Vermin: A Traveler's Bestiary* (tales); *Houseboat on the Ganges & A Room in Kathmandu* (memoir); *Company of Crows* and *Milepost 27* --winner of the Southwest Book of the Year 2019. Visit: marilynstablein.com.

Brett Stout is a 40-year-old artist and writer. He is a high school dropout and former construction worker turned college graduate and paramedic. He creates mostly controversial work, usually while breathing toxic paint fumes from a small cramped apartment known as "The Nerd Lab" in Myrtle Beach, South Carolina. His work has appeared in a vast range of diverse media, from international indie zines like *Litro Magazine UK* to Brown University.

Fabio Tasso was born in Savona, Italy. He accomplished a BFA at the Fine Art Academy of Genoa and an MFA in Carrara, where he developed the first of his sculpt-making processes. During his studies he lived and taught in Nepal, focusing on the connection between emptiness and fullness in art. Since 2015 he has been a professor at the Fine Art Academy of Genoa, teaching Life Drawing, Artistic Anatomy and Sculpture.

D. Harlan Wilson is an American novelist, literary critic, playwright, editor, and university professor. He is the author of over thirty book-length works of fiction and nonfiction, and hundreds of his stories, essays, and reviews have appeared in magazines, journals, and anthologies across the world in multiple languages. Visit him online at www.dharlanwilson.com.

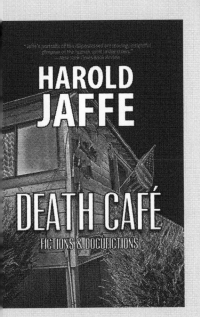
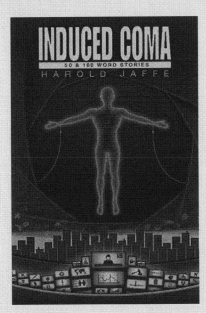

Made in the USA
Monee, IL
24 November 2020